STRANGE NEWS
FROM ANOTHER STAR

Strange News
from Another Star

AND OTHER TALES

HERMANN HESSE

TRANSLATED BY DENVER LINDLEY

Farrar, Straus and Giroux

NEW YORK

Translation copyright © 1972
by Farrar, Straus and Giroux, Inc.

SECOND PRINTING, 1972

Translated from the German, Märchen,
Copyright S. Fischer Verlag, 1919;
Copyright 1955 by Suhrkamp Verlag, Berlin
Library of Congress catalog card number: 70–179791
Published simultaneously in Canada
by Doubleday Canada Ltd., Toronto
Printed in the United States of America

Contents

STRANGE NEWS
FROM ANOTHER STAR

Augustus

A YOUNG WOMAN living in Mostackerstrasse had lost her husband through an accident shortly after their marriage, and she now sat poor and abandoned in her little room, waiting for the child who was destined to be fatherless. And because she was so utterly alone, her thoughts dwelt constantly on the expected child, and there was nothing beautiful and splendid and enviable that she did not plan and wish and dream for the little one. A stone house with plate-glass windows and a fountain in the garden seemed to her just barely good enough for him, and as for his career, he had to become at least a professor or a king.

Next door to poor Frau Elisabeth lived an old man, a little gray fellow who seldom walked abroad and, when he did so, wore a tasseled cap and carried an old-fashioned green umbrella with whalebone ribs. Children were afraid of him and grownups said to one another that he probably had good reason to live in so retired a fashion. Often he would not be seen by anyone for a long time, but sometimes in the evening a delicate music, as though from a great number of tiny, fragile instruments, would drift out of his dilapidated little house. Then the children passing by would ask their mothers whether angels were singing inside, or perhaps fairies, but their mothers knew nothing about such things and would say: "No, no, that must be a music box."

This little man, who was known to his neighbors as Herr Binsswanger, had an odd kind of friendship with Frau Elisabeth. As a matter of fact, they never spoke to each other, but little old Herr Binsswanger bowed in the most friendly fashion every time he went past her window, and she nodded gratefully in return and liked him, and both thought: If things should sometime go very ill with me, then I shall certainly go for help to my neighbor's house. And when it began to grow dark and Frau Elisabeth sat alone at her window and sorrowed for her dead beloved or thought about her little child and fell to dreaming, then Herr Binsswanger would gently open his casement window and out of his dark room flowed comforting music, soft and silvery like moonlight through a rift in the clouds. For her part, Frau Elisabeth tended several old geranium plants growing at his back window; he always forgot to water them but they were always green and full of blossoms and never showed a wilted leaf because Frau Elisabeth took care of them very early every morning.

And now one raw and windy evening when it was getting on toward autumn and no one was abroad in Mostackerstrasse, the poor woman realized that her hour had come and she was frightened because she was entirely alone. But as night fell, an old woman came on foot with a lantern in her hand; she entered the house and boiled water and laid out linens and did everything that is needful when a child is about to come into the world. Frau Elisabeth allowed herself to be looked after in silence, and only when the baby was there, wrapped in fine new swaddling clothes, and had begun his first sleep on earth, did she ask the old woman whence she had come.

"Herr Binsswanger sent me," said the woman, whereupon the weary mother fell asleep; and when she awoke in the morning, milk had been boiled and stood ready for her, everything in the room had been neatly arranged, and beside her lay her little son, screaming because he was hungry; but the old woman was gone. Frau Elisabeth took the baby to her breast and rejoiced that he was so pretty and so strong. She thought of his dead father who had not lived to see him, and tears came to her eyes. But she hugged the little orphan child and smiled once more, then fell asleep again with the little one. When she woke up, there was more milk, a soup had been cooked, and the child was wrapped in clean linens.

Soon the mother was healthy and strong again and could look after herself and little Augustus. She realized then that her son must be christened and that she had no godfather for him. And so toward evening, when twilight had come and the sweet music was once more pouring out of the little house next door, she went over to Herr Binsswanger's. She knocked timidly and was greeted by a cordial cry: "Come in!" The music suddenly ceased, and in the room there was a little old table with a lamp and a book on it, and everything was as normal as could be.

"I have come to thank you," said Frau Elisabeth, "because you sent me that good woman. I wish to pay her too, as soon as I can work again and earn some money. But now I have another worry. The little boy must be christened and is to be named Augustus after his father. But I know no one and I have no godfather for him."

"Yes, I have thought about that too," said her neighbor, stroking his gray beard. "It would be a good thing if he were to have a kind, rich godfather who could look after him if things should ever go badly for you. But I too am lonesome and old and have few friends and so I cannot recommend anyone to you, except perhaps myself, if you would accept me."

This made the poor mother happy, and she thanked the little man and enthusiastically agreed. The next Sunday they carried the baby to the church and had him baptized, and the same old woman appeared there too and gave the child a taler. When Frau Elisabeth did not want to accept it, the old woman said: "No, take it. I am old and have what I need. Perhaps the taler will bring him luck. I was glad for once to do a favor for Herr Binsswanger. We are old friends."

They went back to Frau Elisabeth's room together and she made coffee for her guests. Herr Binsswanger had brought a cake, so it turned into a real baptismal feast. After they had finished eating and drinking and the infant had long since fallen asleep, the old man said diffidently: "Now that I am little Augustus's godfather, I would like to present him with a king's palace and a sackful of gold pieces, but those are things I do not have. I can only add another taler to the one from our neighbor. However, what I can do for him shall be done. Frau Elisabeth, you have certainly wished your little boy all sorts of fine and beautiful things. Now think carefully what seems to you to be the best wish for him, and I will see to it that it comes true. You have one wish for your youngster, whatever one you like, but only one. Consider well, and this evening when you hear my little music box playing, you must whisper your wish into your little one's left ear, then it will be fulfilled."

Thereupon he hastily took his departure and the neighbor woman went away with him, leaving Frau Elisabeth dumfounded, and if the talers had not been there in the crib and the cake on the table, she would have thought it all a dream. She sat down beside the cradle and rocked her child while she meditated and considered many beautiful wishes. At first she planned to make him rich, then handsome, then tremendously strong, then shrewd and clever, but at each choice she felt some hesitation, and finally she concluded that all this was really only the little old man's joke.

It had already grown dark and she had almost fallen asleep sitting beside the cradle, for she was weary from playing hostess, from her troubles and from thinking of so many wishes, when suddenly there drifted over from next door a faint, subtle music, more beautiful and delicate than had ever been heard from a music box. At the sound Frau Elisabeth gave a start and remembered, and now she once more believed in her neighbor Binsswanger and his gift as godfather, but the more she reflected and the more she wanted to make a wish, the more confused her mind became, so that she could not decide upon anything. She was greatly distressed and had tears in her eyes, then the music sounded softer and fainter, and she knew that if she did not make a wish that very instant, it would be too late.

She sighed aloud and bent over her boy and whispered in his left ear: "My little son, I wish for you—I wish for you—" and as the beautiful music became fainter and fainter, she was frightened and said quickly: "—I wish for you that everyone will love you."

The strains had now completely died away and it was deathly still in the dark room. She bent over the cradle and wept and was filled with anxiety and fear, and she cried: "Oh, now that I have wished for you the best thing I knew, perhaps it was not the right thing. And if everyone, every single person, loves you, still no one will ever love you as much as your mother does."

Augustus grew up to be a pretty blond boy with bright, mettlesome eyes whom his mother spoiled and who was well liked by everyone. Frau Elisabeth quickly realized that her christening-day wish for her child was coming true, for the little one was hardly old enough to walk on the streets when everyone he met found him so pretty and pert and clever that they patted his hand and openly admired him. Young mothers smiled at him, old women gave him apples, and if at any time he was naughty, no one believed that he could have done wrong; or if it was obvious that he had, people shrugged their shoulders and said: "You really can't hold anything against that dear little fellow."

People who had noticed the handsome boy came to see his mother, and she who had once been so alone and had had very little sewing work to do, now as the mother of

Augustus had more patrons than she could ever have wished. Things went well with her and with the youngster too, and whenever they went out walking together, the neighbors smiled and bowed to them and turned to look after the lucky boy.

What was best of all happened to Augustus next door at his godfather's. Herr Binsswanger would sometimes call him over to his house in the evening when it was dark and the only light in the room was the little red fire burning in the black hollow of the fireplace. The old man would draw the child down beside him on a fur rug on the floor and would tell him long stories as they both stared at the quiet flames. Occasionally, when a long story was at an end and the little boy had grown very sleepy staring with half-open eyes at the fire in the dark silence, then out of the darkness flowed sweet polyphonic music, and when the two had listened to it for a long time in silence, it often happened that the whole room was suddenly filled with tiny sparkling cherubs who flew in circles on bright golden wings, dancing elaborately about one another in pairs and singing at the same time. The whole room resounded in a hundredfold harmony of joy and serene beauty. It was the loveliest thing Augustus had ever experienced, and when later on he thought of his childhood, it was the dark, quiet room of his old godfather and the red flames in the fireplace and the music and the festive, golden, magic flight of the angelic beings that filled his memory and made him homesick.

As the boy grew older, there were times when his mother was sad and felt compelled to think back to that baptismal night. Augustus ran merrily about in the nearby streets and was welcome everywhere. People gave him nuts and pears, cookies and toys, all kinds of good things to eat and drink, set him on their knees, let him pick flowers in their gardens, and often he did not get home until late in the evening and would angrily push aside his mother's soup. If she then was unhappy and wept, he would look bored and go sullenly to his cot. If she scolded or punished him, he screamed and loudly complained that everyone except his mother was nice and kind to him. She was often seriously angry at her son at these troubled times, but later, as he lay sleeping among his pillows and the light of her candle shimmered on his innocent, childish face, then all harshness left her heart, and she would kiss him cautiously so as not to awaken him. It was *her* fault that everyone loved Augustus, and sometimes she thought with sorrow and almost with dread that perhaps it would have been better had she never made that wish.

Once she happened to be standing beside Herr Binsswanger's geranium window, cutting the withered leaves from the plants with a small pair of shears, when she heard the voice of her son in the courtyard that lay behind the two houses, and turned around to look for him. He was leaning against the wall with a disdainful look on his pretty face, and in front of him stood a girl taller than he was, saying coaxingly: "Come now, you'll be nice, won't you, and give me a kiss?"

"I don't want to," Augustus said, putting his hands in his pockets.

"Oh, please do,'" she said again. "I'll give you something nice."

"What will you give me?" the boy asked.

"I have two apples," she said timidly.

"I don't want any apples," he said contemptuously and started to leave.

But the girl caught hold of his arm and said cajolingly: "Wait, I have a beautiful ring too."

"Let's see it!" Augustus said.

She showed him her ring, and he looked at it carefully, then took it off her finger and put it on his own, held it up to the light and nodded approvingly.

"All right then, you can have a kiss," he said carelessly, and gave the girl a hasty peck on the mouth.

"You'll come and play with me now, won't you?" she said confidently, taking his arm.

But he pushed her aside and shouted rudely: "Leave me in peace, can't you? I have others to play with." The girl began to cry and stole out of the courtyard. He looked after her with a bored and exasperated expression, then he turned the ring around on his finger and examined it. He began to whistle and walked slowly away.

His mother stood still with her gardening shears in her hand, shocked at the harshness and contempt with which her child had treated another's love. She turned away from the flowers and shook her head and said over and over to herself: "Why, he's bad, he has no heart at all."

When Augustus came home a short time later, she took him to task, but he looked at her laughingly with his blue eyes and showed no sign of guilt. Then he began to sing and he was so affectionate with her, so funny and charming and tender, that she had to laugh, and she decided that with children one need not necessarily take everything so seriously.

But the youngster did not entirely escape punishment for his misdeeds. His godfather Binsswanger was the only one for whom Augustus felt any regard, and in the evening when he went to see him his godfather would say: "Today no fire is burning on the hearth and there is no music, the little angel children are sad because you were so bad." The boy would go home in silence and throw himself on his bed and weep, and for many days afterward he would try hard to be good and kind.

Nevertheless, the fire on the hearth burned less and less often, nor could his godfather be bribed with tears or caresses. By the time Augustus was twelve years old, the enchanting, angelic flight in his godfather's room had already become a distant dream, and if by chance he did actually dream about it in the night, then on the following day he would be doubly wild and boisterous and order his many friends about with the ruthlessness of a field marshal.

His mother had long since grown tired of hearing from everyone how fine and charming her boy was; she had, in fact, nothing but trouble with him. And when one day his teacher came to her and said he knew of someone willing to enter her son in a distant school, she went next door and had a talk with her neighbor. Soon thereafter on a spring morning a carriage drew up and Augustus in a fine new suit got in and said farewell to his mother and his godfather and all the neighbors because he was to travel to the capital and study there. His mother had neatly parted his blond hair for the last time, had given him her blessing, and now the horses moved off and Augustus rode away into the great world.

Many years later when Augustus was a college student and wore a red cap and a mustache, he traveled back once more by carriage to his home town because his godfather had written that his mother was very ill and could not live long. The youth arrived in the evening, and people were amazed to see him get out of the carriage followed by the coachman, who carried a big leather trunk into the house. Frau Elisabeth lay dying in the old low-ceilinged room, and when the handsome student saw her looking white and withered on the white pillows, only able to greet him with her quiet eyes, he sank down weeping by the bed; and he kissed his mother's chill hands and knelt beside her the whole night through, until the hands had grown cold and the eyes lifeless.

And when his mother had been buried, his godfather Binsswanger took him by the arm and led him into his little house, which seemed to the young man even shabbier and darker than before, and when they had sat together for a long time and only the small window shimmered feebly in the darkness, then the little old man stroked his gray beard with his thin fingers and said to Augustus: "I will make a fire on the hearth, then we won't need the lamp. I know you must leave tomorrow, and now that your mother is dead, you won't be back again very soon."

So saying, he kindled a small fire on the hearth, pulled his chair near it, and arranged Augustus's chair close to his own. They sat thus together for another long while, looking into the glowing coals, until the flying sparks had grown sparse, and then the old man said softly: "Farewell, Augustus, I wish you well. You had a fine mother who did more for you than you know. I would gladly have made music for you again and shown you the small blessed ones, but you know that isn't possible any more. But you must not forget them and you must remember that they always continue to sing and that perhaps you will be able to hear them once more if a time comes when you desire it with a lonely and longing heart. Now give me your hand, my boy, I am old and must go to bed."

Augustus shook hands with him but could not speak. He went sadly over to the deserted little house and for the last time lay down to sleep in his old home, but before falling asleep he thought he heard again, very far off and faint, the sweet music of his childhood. Next morning he left, and for a long time nothing was heard of him in his home town.

Soon, too, he forgot his Godfather Binsswanger and the angels. He lived a life of luxury and reveled in it. No one could equal his style as he rode through the streets waving to adoring girls and teasing them with secret glances, no one could drive a four-in-hand with such gaiety and elegance, no one was as boisterous and boastful through a summer night's drinking bout in the garden. The rich widow whose lover he was gave him money and clothes and horses and everything he needed or wanted, he traveled with her to Paris and to Rome and slept in her silken sheets. His beloved, however, was the soft, blond daughter of a burgher; he met her recklessly in her father's garden, and she wrote him long, ardent letters when he was abroad.

But the time came when he did not return. He had found friends in Paris, and because his rich mistress had begun to bore him and study had long since become a nuisance, he stayed abroad and lived the life of high society. He kept horses, dogs, women, lost money and won money in great golden rolls, and everywhere people pursued him, were captivated by him and served him, and he smiled and accepted it all, just as he had accepted the young girl's ring long before. The magic of his mother's wish lay in his eyes and on his lips, women smothered him with tenderness, friends raved about him, and no one saw—he scarcely noticed it himself—that his heart had grown empty and greedy and that his soul was sick and full of pain. At times he grew tired of being loved so by everyone and went alone in disguise to foreign cities, but everywhere he found people fatuous and all too easy to conquer, everywhere he scorned the love that followed him so ardently and was content with so little. He often felt disgust for men and women because they did not have more pride, and he spent whole days alone with his dogs in the beautiful hunting preserves in the mountains; a stag stalked and shot made him happier than the conquest of a beautiful spoiled woman.

Then in the course of a sea voyage he chanced to meet the young wife of an ambassador, a reserved, slender lady of the northern nobility who stood out with marked distinction among the many fashionable women and worldly men. She was proud and quiet, as though no one was her equal, and when he watched her and saw that her glance seemed to brush past him too, hastily and indifferently, it seemed to him as though he were experiencing for the very first time what love is, and he determined to win her heart. From then on, at every hour of the day, he stayed close to her and in her sight, and because he himself was always surrounded by people who admired him and sought his society, he and the beautiful, unmoved lady were always at the center of the company of travelers, like a prince with his princess; even the blonde's husband treated him with deference and took pains to please him.

It was never possible for him to be alone with the lovely stranger until in a southern port the whole party of travelers left the ship in order to spend a few hours wandering around in the foreign city and feeling earth under their feet again. He did not move from his beloved's side and presently, in the colorful confusion of a marketplace, he succeeded in detaining her in conversation. Innumerable little dark alleys entered this square, into one of which he led her; she accompanied him trustfully, but when she suddenly found herself alone with him she became nervous and looked all around for their traveling companions.

He turned to her passionately, took her reluctant hand in his, and besought her to leave the ship with him and flee.

The young woman grew pale and kept her eyes fixed on the ground. "Oh, that is not chivalrous," she said softly. "Allow me to forget what you have just said."

"I am no knight," cried Augustus. "I am a lover, and a lover knows nothing except his beloved and has no thought except to be with her. O fair lady, flee with me, we will be happy."

She looked at him solemnly and reproachfully with her clear blue eyes. "How could you know," she whispered sadly, "that I loved you? I cannot deny it; I love you and I have often wished that you might be my husband. For you are the first I have ever loved with all my heart. Alas, how can love go so far astray! I would never have thought it possible for me to love a man who is not pure and good. But I prefer a thousand times to stay with my husband, whom I do not greatly love but who is a knight full of honor and chivalry, qualities that are foreign to you. And now do not say another word, but take me back to the ship; otherwise, I will call out to strangers to protect me against your insolence."

And no matter how much he stormed and pled with her, she turned away from him and would have walked on alone if he had not silently gone after her and accompanied her to the ship. There he had his trunk taken ashore without saying goodbye to anyone.

From then on, the luck of this much loved man changed. Virtue and honor had become hateful to him, he trod them underfoot and diverted himself by seducing vir-

tuous women through his magical wiles and exploiting un-
suspecting men whom he quickly made his friends and
then contemptuously cast off. He reduced women and
girls to poverty and forthwith disowned them, he sought
out youths from noble houses whom he seduced and cor-
rupted. There was no pleasure that he did not indulge in
and exhaust, no vice that he did not cultivate and then
discard. But there was no longer any joy in his heart, and
to the love that greeted him everywhere no echo responded in his soul.

Sullen and morose, he lived in a magnificent country
house on the seacoast, and the men and women who visited him there he tormented with the wildest whims and
spitefulness. He took delight in degrading people and treat-
ing them with complete contempt; he was satiated and
disgusted with the unsought, unwanted, undeserved love
that surrounded him, he felt the worthlessness of a squan-
dered and disordered life in which he had never given but
always simply taken. Sometimes he went hungry for a
long time just to be able to feel a real appetite again, to
satisfy a desire.

The news spread among his friends that he was ill and
needed peace and solitude. Letters came but he never
read them, and worried people inquired of his servants
about his state of health. But he sat alone and deeply
troubled in his hall above the sea, his life lay empty and
desolate behind him, as barren and devoid of love as the
billowing gray salt sea. His face was hideous as he huddled there in his chair at the high window, holding an ac-
counting with himself. White gulls swept by on the coast

wind, he followed them with eyes empty of all joy and sympathy. As he reached the conclusion of his meditations and summoned his valet, only his lips moved in a harsh and evil smile. He ordered that all his friends be invited to a feast on a given day, but his intention was to terrify and mock them on their arrival with the sight of an empty house and his own corpse. For he was determined to end his life by poison.

On the evening before the appointed feast he sent his whole staff of servants from the house, and the great rooms fell completely silent. He withdrew to his bedchamber, where he mixed a powerful poison in a glass of Cyprus wine and raised it to his lips.

But just as he was about to drink, there was a knocking at the door, and when he did not reply, the door opened and a little old man entered. He went straight up to Augustus and carefully took the full glass out of his hands, and a familiar voice said: "Good evening, Augustus, how are things going with you?"

Astounded, angered, but also ashamed, Augustus smiled mockingly and said: "Herr Binsswanger, are you still alive? It has been a long time, and you actually do not seem to have grown any older. But at the moment you are disturbing me, my dear fellow. I am tired and was just about to take a sleeping potion."

"So I see," his godfather replied calmly. "You are going to take a sleeping potion and you are right, this is the last wine that can still help you. But before that we'll chat for a minute, my boy, and since I have a long journey behind me, you won't mind if I refresh myself with a small drink."

Whereupon he took the glass and raised it to his lips and, before Augustus could restrain him, tilted it up and drained it at a single gulp.

Augustus became deathly pale. He sprang toward his godfather, shook him by the shoulders, and cried sharply: "Old man, do you know what you have just drunk?"

Herr Binsswanger nodded his clever gray head and smiled. "It's Cyprus wine, I see, and it's not bad. You don't seem to be in want. But I haven't much time and I won't detain you for long if you will just listen to me."

Disconcerted, Augustus stared into his godfather's bright eyes with horror, expecting to see him collapse at any instant.

But Herr Binsswanger simply sat down comfortably on a chair and nodded benignly at his young friend.

"Are you worried for fear this drink of wine will hurt me? Now just relax. It's nice of you to be worried about me. I would never have expected it. But now let's talk again as we used to in the old days. It seems to me that you have become satiated with a life of frivolity? I can understand that, and when I leave, you can refill your glass and drink it down. But before that I must tell you something."

Augustus leaned against the wall and listened to the little old man's good, kind voice, a voice so familiar to him from childhood that it awoke echoes of the past in his soul. Deep shame and sorrow overcame him as he looked back at his own innocent youth.

"I have drunk your poison," the old man went on, "because I am the one who is responsible for your misery. At your christening your mother made a wish for you and I fulfilled it for her, even though it was a foolish wish. There is no need for you to be told what it was; it has become a curse, as you yourself have realized. I am sorry it turned out this way, and it would certainly make me happy if I could live to see you sitting beside me once more, at home in front of the hearth, listening to the little angels singing. That is not easy, and at the moment perhaps it seems to you impossible that your heart could ever again be healthy and pure and cheerful. But it is possible, and I want to beg you to attempt it. Your poor mother's wish did not suit you well, Augustus. How would it be now if you allowed me to fulfill a wish for you too, any wish? Very likely you will not want money or possessions or power or the love of women, of which you have had enough. Think carefully, and if you believe you know a magic spell that could make your wasted life fairer and better, that could make you happy once more, then wish it for yourself."

Augustus sat deep in thought and was silent, but he was too exhausted and hopeless, and so after a while he said: "I thank you, Godfather Binsswanger, but I believe there is no comb that can smooth out the tangles of my life. It is better for me to do what I was planning to do when you came in. But I thank you, nevertheless, for coming."

"Yes," said the aged man thoughtfully, "I can imagine that this is not easy for you. But perhaps you can take thought once more, Augustus, perhaps you will realize what is now principally lacking, or perhaps you can remember those times when your mother was still alive and when you occasionally came to see me in the evening. After all, you were sometimes happy, were you not?"

"Yes, in those days," Augustus said, nodding, and the image of his radiant youth looked back at him from afar, palely as though out of an antique mirror. "But that cannot come again. I cannot wish to be a child once more. Why, then it would begin all over again!"

"No, you are quite right, that would make no sense. But think once more of the time when we were together back at home, and of the poor girl whom you used to visit at night in her father's garden when you were at college, and think too of the beautiful fair-haired lady with whom you once traveled on a ship at sea, and think of all the moments when you have ever been happy and when life seemed to you good and precious. Perhaps you can recognize what made you happy at those times and can wish for it. Do so for my sake, my boy!"

Augustus closed his eyes and looked back over his life as one looks back from a dark corridor toward a distant point of light, and he saw again how everything had once been bright and beautiful around him and then had become dimmer and dimmer until he stood now in complete darkness, and nothing could any longer cheer him. And the more he thought back and remembered, the more beautiful and lovable and desirable seemed that little glowing light, and finally he recognized it and tears started from his eyes.

"I will try," he said to his godfather. "Take away the old magic which has not helped me and give me instead the ability to love people!"

Weeping, he knelt before his ancient friend and even as he sank down he felt his love for this aged man burning within him and struggling for expression in forgotten words and gestures. His godfather, that tiny man, took him up in his arms, carried him to the bed and laid him down, and stroked his hair and feverish brow.

"That is good," he whispered to him softly. "That is good, my child, all will be well."

Thereupon Augustus felt himself overwhelmed by a crushing weariness, as though he had aged many years in an instant. He fell into a deep sleep, and the old man went silently out of the empty house.

Augustus was awakened by a wild uproar resounding through the house, and when he got up and opened his bedchamber door he found the hall and all the rooms filled with the friends who had come to his party and found the place deserted. They were angry and disappointed, and when he went toward them, intending to win them all back as usual with a smile and a joke, he suddenly realized that the power to do this had gone from him. They had barely caught sight of him when they all began to scream at him. He smiled helplessly and stretched out appealing hands in self-defense, but they fell upon him raging.

"You cheat," one man cried. "Where is the money you owe me?" And another: "And the horse I loaned you?" And a beautiful furious woman: "Everybody knows my secrets now because you've talked about me everywhere. Oh, how I hate you, you monster!" And a hollow-eyed young man shrieked, his face distorted with hatred: "You know what you have made of me, you fiend, you corrupter of youth!"

And so it went, each one heaping insults and curses on him—all of them justified—and many striking him; and after they had left, breaking mirrors as they went and taking many valuables away with them, Augustus got up from the floor, beaten and humiliated. When he entered his bedchamber and looked in the mirror while washing, his face peered out at him, wrinkled and ugly, the eyes red and watering, and blood was dripping from his forehead.

"That's my reward," he said to himself, as he rinsed the blood from his face, and hardly had he had time to reflect a little when uproar broke out once more in the house and a crowd came storming up the stairway: moneylenders to whom he had mortgaged his house; a husband whose wife he had seduced; fathers whose sons he had tempted into vice and misery; maids and menservants he had dismissed, policemen and lawyers. An hour later he sat handcuffed in a patrol wagon on his way to jail. Behind him the crowd shouted and sang mocking songs, and a street hoodlum threw a handful of filth through the window into the prisoner's face.

Then the city reechoed with the shameful deeds of this man whom so many had known and loved. There was no sin he was not accused of, none that he denied. People he had long since forgotten stood before the judges and accused him of things he had done years before: servants he had rewarded and who had robbed him revealed his secret vices, every face was full of loathing and hatred, and there was no one to speak in his defense, to praise him, to exonerate him, to recall any good thing about him.

He did not protest against any of this but allowed himself to be led into a cell and out of it again and before the judges and witnesses. He looked with amazement and sorrow out of sick eyes at the many evil, angry, hate-filled faces, and in each he saw under the hatred and distortion a hidden charm and felt a spark of affection. All these people had once loved him, and he had loved none of them; now he begged their forgiveness and sought to remember something good about each one of them.

In the end he was sent to prison, and no one ventured to visit him. Then in his feverish dreams he talked to his mother and to his first beloved, to his Godfather Binsswanger and the northern lady on the ship, and when he awoke and sat lonely and abandoned through the fearful days, he suffered all the pains of longing and isolation and he yearned for the sight of people as he had never yearned for any pleasure or possession.

And when he was released from prison, he was sick and old and no one any longer recognized him. The world went its way; people rode in carriages and on horseback and promenaded in the streets; fruits and flowers, toys and newspapers were offered for sale; and no one turned to speak to Augustus. Beautiful women whom he had once held in his arms in an atmosphere of music and champagne went by in their equipages, and the dust of their passing settled over Augustus.

But the dreadful emptiness and loneliness that had stifled him in the midst of luxury now had completely disappeared. When he paused in the shadow of a gateway to take shelter for a moment from the heat of the sun, or when he begged a drink of water in the courtyard of some modest dwelling, then he was amazed at how sullenly and ill-temperedly people treated him, the same people who had earlier responded to his proud and indifferent words gratefully and with sparkling eyes. Nevertheless, he was delighted and touched and moved by the sight of everyone, he loved the children he saw at play and going to school, and he loved the old people sitting on benches in front of their little houses, warming their withered hands in the sun. If he saw some young man following a girl with yearning glances or a worker returning on a holiday eve and picking up his children in his arms, or a clever, fashionable doctor driving by in silence and haste, intent upon his patients, or equally some poor, ill-clad trollop waiting by a lamppost, ready to offer even him, the outcast, her love, then all these were his brothers and sisters and each one was stamped with the memory of a beloved mother and some finer background, or the secret sign of a higher and nobler destiny, and each was dear and remarkable in his eyes and gave him food for thought, and he considered that no one was worse than himself.

Augustus decided to wander through the world and look for a place where he could be of some service to people and thus show them his love. He had to get used to the fact that his appearance no longer made anyone happy; his cheeks had fallen in, his clothes and shoes were those of a beggar, even his voice and gait had none of the engaging quality that had once cheered and delighted the populace. Children feared him because of his scraggly, long gray beard, the well-dressed shunned his company because he made them feel soiled and infected, and the poor distrusted him as a stranger who might try to snatch away their few morsels of food. And so it was hard for him to be of service to anyone. But he learned, and he allowed nothing to offend him. He helped a little child stretching out his hand for the latch of a shop which he could not reach, and sometimes there would be someone even worse off than himself, a lame man or a blind man whom he could assist and cheer a little along his road. And when he could not do that, he cheerfully gave what little he had, a bright encouraging glance and a brotherly greeting, a look of understanding and sympathy. He learned in his wanderings to tell from people's expressions what they expected of him, what would give them pleasure: for one, a loud cheerful greeting; for another, a quiet glance; or when someone wanted to be left alone, to be undisturbed. He was amazed each day at how much misery there was in the world and how content people could be nevertheless, and it was splendid and heartening to him always to find every sorrow followed by laughter, next to each death knell a child's song, next to every greed and baseness an act of courtesy, a joke, a comforting word, a smile.

Human life seemed to him marvelously well arranged. If he turned a corner and a horde of schoolboys came bounding toward him, he saw how courage and living joy and the beauty of youth shone in all their eyes, and if they teased him and tormented him a little, that was not so bad; it was even understandable. When he caught sight of himself in a store window or the pool of a drinking fountain, he saw that he was very wrinkled and shabby. No, for him it could no longer be a question of pleasing people or wielding power, he had had enough of that. It was most edifying to see how others struggled along those paths he had once followed and believed they were making progress, and how everyone pursued his goal so eagerly and with so much vigor and pride and joy—in his eyes this was a wonderful drama.

Now winter came and then summer once more, and Augustus lay ill for a long time in a charity hospital, and here he enjoyed, silently and thankfully, the pleasure of seeing wretched folk clinging tenaciously to life and triumphing over death. It was marvelous to see the patience in the faces of those gravely ill, and in the eyes of convalescents the increasing bright joy of life, and beautiful too were the calm, dignified faces of the dead, and fairer than all these were the love and patience of the pretty, immaculate nurses. But this period too came to an end, the autumn wind blew, and Augustus wandered forth in the face of winter. A strange impatience took possession of him, now that he saw how infinitely slow his progress was, for he still wanted to visit all sorts of places and to look into so many, many people's eyes. His hair had turned gray and his eyes smiled weakly behind red, inflamed lids; gradually his memory too grew clouded so that it seemed to him as though he had never seen the world other than it was on that day. But he was content with it and found it altogether splendid and deserving of love.

At the beginning of winter, he came to a city. Snow was drifting through the dark streets, and a few belated street urchins threw snowballs at the wanderer, but otherwise an evening hush hung over everything. Augustus was feeling very weary when he came to a narrow street that seemed familiar, and then another as well. And there he was, standing in front of his mother's house and that of his Godfather Binsswanger, both of them small and shabby in the cold driving snow; but his godfather's one window was bright shimmering red and friendly in the winter night.

Augustus went in and knocked at the living-room door. The little old man came to meet him and led him silently into the room, where it was warm and quiet, with a bright little fire burning on the hearth.

"Are you hungry?" his godfather asked.

But Augustus was not hungry, he only smiled and shook his head.

"But you must be tired," his godfather said, spreading his old fur rug on the floor, and the two old people huddled there close to each other and looked into the fire.

"You have come a long way," his godfather said.

"Oh, it was beautiful. I'm just tired now. May I sleep here? Then I will go on tomorrow."

"Indeed, you may. But don't you want to see the angels dance once more?"

"The angels? Oh, yes, that's something I would dearly love, if I could be a child again."

"We haven't seen each other in a long time," his godfather went on. "You have become so good-looking, your eyes are again as kind and gentle as they were in the old times when your mother was still alive. It was good of you to visit me."

The wanderer in his torn clothes sat quietly beside his friend. He had never before been so weary, and the pleasant warmth and the glow of the fire made his head swim so that he could no longer distinguish clearly between that day and earlier times.

"Godfather Binsswanger," he said, "I've been naughty again and at home Mother cried. You must talk to her and tell her I'm going to be good from now on. Will you?"

"I will," his godfather said. "But don't worry, she loves you."

Now the fire had burned down and Augustus was staring into the dim redness with large, sleep-filled eyes as he had done in his childhood. His godfather took his head in his lap, a delicate eerie music drifted softly and enchantingly through the darkened room, and a thousand pairs of tiny glittering spirits hovered and circled happily about one another in elaborate arabesques in the air. Augustus watched and listened and opened wide all his child's receptive sense to this regained paradise.

Once it seemed to him that his mother called, but he was too weary, and after all his godfather had promised to speak to her. And when he had fallen asleep, his godfather folded his hands and sat listening beside the silenced heart until complete darkness filled the room.

The Poet

THE STORY is told of the Chinese poet Han Fook that
from early youth he was animated by an intense desire to learn all about the poet's art and to perfect himself
in everything connected with it. In those days he was still
living in his home city on the Yellow River and had
become engaged—at his own wish and with the aid of his
parents, who loved him tenderly—to a girl of good family;
the wedding was to be announced shortly for a chosen day
of good omen. Han Fook at this time was about twenty
years old and a handsome young man, modest and of
agreeable manners, instructed in the sciences and, despite
his youth, already known among the literary folk of his
district for a number of remarkable poems. Without being
exactly rich, he had the expectation of comfortable
means, which would be increased by the dowry of his
bride, and since this bride was also very beautiful and vir-
tuous, nothing whatever seemed lacking to the youth's
happiness. Nevertheless, he was not entirely content, for
his heart was filled with the ambition to become a perfect
poet.

Then one evening when a lantern festival was being
celebrated on the river, it happened that Han Fook was
wandering alone on the opposite bank. He leaned against
the trunk of a tree that hung out over the water, and mir-

rored in the river he saw a thousand lights floating and trembling, he saw men and women and young girls on the boats and barges, greeting each other and glowing like beautiful flowers in their festive robes, he heard the girl singers, the hum of the zither and the sweet tones of the flute players, and over all this he saw the bluish night arched like the dome of a temple. The youth's heart beat high as he took in all this beauty, a lonely observer in pursuit of his whim. But much as he longed to go across the river and take part in the feast and be in the company of his bride-to-be and his friends, much deeper was his longing to absorb it all as a perceptive observer and to reproduce it in a wholly perfect poem: the blue of the night and the play of light on the water and the joy of the guests and the yearning of the silent onlooker leaning against the tree trunk on the bank. He realized that at all festivals and with all joys of this earth he would never feel wholly comfortable and serene at heart; even in the midst of life he would remain solitary and be, to a certain extent, a watcher, an alien, and he felt that his soul, unlike most others, was so formed that he must be alone to experience both the beauty of the earth and the secret longings of a stranger. Thereupon he grew sad, and pondered this matter, and the conclusion of his thoughts was this, that true happiness and deep satisfaction could only be his if on occasion he succeeded in mirroring the world so perfectly in his poems that in these mirror images he would possess the essence of the world, purified and made eternal.

Han Fook hardly knew whether he was still awake or

had fallen asleep when he heard a slight rustling and saw a stranger standing beside the trunk of the tree, an old man of reverend aspect, wearing a violet robe. Han Fook roused himself and greeted the stranger with the salutation appropriate to the aged and distinguished; the stranger, however, smiled and spoke a few verses in which everything the young man had just felt was expressed so completely and beautifully and so exactly in accord with the rules of the great poets that the youth's heart stood still with amazement.

"Oh, who are you?" he cried, bowing deeply. "You who can see into my soul and who recite more beautiful verses than I have ever heard from any of my teachers!"

The stranger smiled once more with the smile of one made perfect, and said: "If you wish to be a poet, come to me. You will find my hut beside the source of the Great River in the northwestern mountains. I am called Master of the Perfect Word."

Thereupon the aged man stepped into the narrow shadow of the tree and instantly disappeared, and Han Fook, searching for him in vain and finding no trace of him, finally decided that it had all been a dream caused by his fatigue. He hastened across to the boats and joined in the festival, but amid the conversation and the music of the flutes he continued to hear the mysterious voice of the stranger, and his soul seemed to have gone away with the old man, for he sat remote and with dreaming eyes among the merry folk, who teased him for being in love.

A few days later Han Fook's father prepared to summon his friends and relations to decide upon the day of the wedding. The bridegroom demurred and said: "Forgive me if I seem to offend against the duty a son owes his father. But you know how great my longing is to distinguish myself in the art of poetry, and even though some of my friends praise my poems, nevertheless I know very well that I am still a beginner and still on the first stage of the journey. Therefore, I beg you to let me go my way in loneliness for a while and devote myself to my studies, for it seems to me that having a wife and a house to govern will keep me from these things. But now I am still young and without other duties, and I would like to live for a time for my poetry, from which I hope to gain joy and fame."

This speech filled his father with great surprise and he said: "This art must indeed be dearer to you than anything, since you wish to postpone your wedding on account of it. Or has something arisen between you and your bride? If so, tell me so that I can help to reconcile you, or select another girl."

The son swore, however, that his bride-to-be was no less dear to him than she had been yesterday and always, and that no shadow of discord had fallen between them. Then he told his father that on the day of the lantern festival a Master had become known to him in a dream, and that he desired to be his pupil more ardently than all the happiness in the world.

"Very well," his father said, "I will grant you a year. In this time you may pursue your dream, which perhaps was sent to you by a god."

"It may even take two years," Han Fook said hesitantly. "Who can tell?"

So his father let him go, and was troubled; the youth, however, wrote a letter to his bride, said farewell, and departed.

When he had wandered for a very long time, he reached the source of the river, and in complete isolation he found a bamboo hut, and in front of the hut on a woven mat sat the aged man whom he had seen beside the tree on the river bank. He sat playing a lute, and when he saw his guest approach with reverence he did not rise or greet him but simply smiled and let his delicate fingers run over the strings, and a magical music flowed like a silver cloud through the valley, so that the youth stood amazed and in his sweet astonishment forgot everything, until the Master of the Perfect Word laid aside his little lute and stepped into the hut. Then Han Fook followed him reverently and stayed with him as his servant and pupil.

With the passing of a month he had learned to despise all the poems he had hitherto composed, and he blotted them out of his memory. And after more months he blotted out all the songs that he had learned from his teachers at home. The Master rarely spoke to him; in silence he taught him the art of lute playing until the pupil's being was entirely saturated with music. Once Han Fook made a little poem which described the flight of two birds in the autumn sky, and he was pleased with it. He dared not show it to the Master, but one evening he sang it outside the hut, and the Master listened attentively. However, he said no word. He simply played softly on his lute and at once the air grew cool and twilight fell suddenly, a sharp wind arose although it was midsummer, and through the sky which had grown gray flew two herons in majestic migration, and everything was so much more beautiful and perfect than in the pupil's verses that the latter became sad and was silent and felt that he was worthless. And this is what the ancient did each time, and when a year had passed, Han Fook had almost completely mastered the playing of the lute, but the art of poetry seemed to him ever more difficult and sublime.

When two years had passed, the youth felt a devouring homesickness for his family, his native city, and his bride, and he besought the Master to let him leave.

The Master smiled and nodded. "You are free," he said, "and may go where you like. You may return, you may stay away, just as it suits you."

Then the pupil set out on his journey and traveled uninterruptedly until one morning in the half light of dawn he stood on the bank of his native river and looked across the arched bridge to his home city. He stole secretly into his father's garden and listened through the window of the bedchamber to his father's breathing as he slept, and he slipped into the orchard beside his bride's house and climbed a pear tree, and from there he saw his bride standing in her room combing her hair. And while he compared all these things which he was seeing with his eyes to the mental pictures he had painted of them in his homesickness, it became clear to him that he was, after all, destined to be a poet, and he saw that in poets' dreams reside a beauty and enchantment that one seeks in vain in the things of the real world. And he climbed down from the tree and fled out of the garden and over the bridge, away from his native city, and returned to the high mountain valley. There, as before, sat the old Master in front of his hut on his modest mat, striking the lute with his fingers, and instead of a greeting he recited two verses about the blessings of art, and at their depth and harmony the young man's eyes filled with tears.

Once more Han Fook stayed with the Master of the Perfect Word, who, now that his pupil had mastered the lute, instructed him in the zither, and the months melted away like snow before the west wind. Twice more it happened that he was overcome by homesickness. On the one occasion he ran away secretly at night, but before he had reached the last bend in the valley the night wind blew across the zither hanging at the door of the hut, and the notes flew after him and called him back so that he could not resist them. But the next time he dreamed he was planting a young tree in his garden, and his wife and children were assembled there and his children were watering the tree with wine and milk. When he awoke, the moon was shining into his room and he got up, disturbed in mind, and saw in the next room the Master lying asleep with his gray beard trembling gently; then he was overcome by a bitter hatred for this man who, it seemed to him, had destroyed his life and cheated him of his future. He was about to throw himself upon the Master and murder him when the ancient opened his eyes and began to smile with a sad sweetness and gentleness that disarmed his pupil.

"Remember, Han Fook," the aged man said softly, "you are free to do what you like. You may go to your home and plant trees, you may hate me and kill me, it makes very little difference."

"Oh, how could I hate you?" the poet cried, deeply moved. "That would be like hating heaven itself."

And he stayed and learned to play the zither, and after that the flute, and later he began under his Master's guidance to make poems, and he slowly learned the secret art of apparently saying only simple and homely things but thereby stirring the hearer's soul like wind on the surface of the water. He described the coming of the sun, how it hesitates on the mountain's rim, and the noiseless darting of the fishes when they flee like shadows under the water, and the swaying of a young birch tree in the spring wind, and when people listened it was not only the sun and the play of the fish and the whispering of the birch tree, but it seemed as though heaven and earth each time chimed together for an instant in perfect harmony, and each hearer was impelled to think with joy or pain about what he loved or hated, the boy about sport, the youth about his beloved, and the old man about death.

Han Fook no longer knew how many years he had spent with the Master beside the source of the Great River; often it seemed to him as though he had entered this valley only the evening before and been received by the ancient playing on his stringed instrument; often, too, it seemed as though all the ages and epochs of man had vanished behind him and become unreal.

And then one morning he awoke alone in the house, and though he searched everywhere and called, the Master had disappeared. Overnight it seemed suddenly to have become autumn, a raw wind tugged at the old hut, and over the ridge of the mountain great flights of migratory birds were moving, though it was not yet the season for that.

Then Han Fook took the little lute with him and descended to his native province, and when he came among men they greeted him with the salutation appropriate to the aged and distinguished, and when he came to his home city he found that his father and his bride and his relations had died and other people were living in their houses. In the evening, however, the festival of the lanterns was celebrated on the river and the poet Han Fook stood on the far side on the darker bank, leaning against the trunk of an ancient tree. And when he played on the little lute, the women began to sigh and looked into the night, enchanted and overwhelmed, and the young men called for the lute player, whom they could not find anywhere, and they exclaimed that none of them had ever heard such tones from a lute. But Han Fook only smiled. He looked into the river where floated the mirrored images of the thousand lamps; and just as he could no longer distinguish between the reflections and reality, so he found in his soul no difference between this festival and that first one when he had stood there as a youth and heard the words of the strange Master.

Flute Dream

H ERE," said my father, handing me a small ivory flute, "take this and don't forget your old father when you are entertaining people in foreign lands with your playing. It is now high time for you to see the world and gain knowledge. I had this flute made for you because you don't like any other kind of work and always just want to sing. Only be sure always to choose bright, cheery songs, otherwise it would be a pity about the gift God has given you."

My dear father understood little about music, he was a scholar; he thought all I had to do was blow into the pretty little flute and that would be that. I did not wish to undeceive him, and so I gave him my thanks, put the flute in my pocket, and took my departure.

Our valley was familiar to me only as far as the big farm mill; and so beyond that the world began, and it pleased me greatly. A bee, tired from flying about, had lighted on my sleeve; I took her with me so that later on at my first resting place I would have a messenger ready to send back home with my greetings.

Woods and meadows accompanied me on my way and the river ran merrily beside me; I saw that the world was little different from my home. The trees and flowers, the ears of corn, and the hazel bushes spoke to me, I sang their songs with them and they understood me just as at home; the singing wakened my bee, she crept slowly up to my shoulder, flew off and circled twice around me with her deep, sweet buzzing, then steered straight as an arrow back toward home.

Presently a young girl came strolling out of the woods carrying a basket on her arm and wearing a broad shade hat of straw on her blond head.

"Grüss Gott," I said to her, "where are you off to?"

"I'm taking the harvesters their dinner," she said, walking beside me. "And where are you going today?"

"I am going out into the world, my father sent me. He thinks I ought to give concerts on the flute, but I don't really know how, I shall have to learn first."

"Well now. And what can you really do? Everyone has to be able to do something, after all."

"Nothing special. I can sing songs."

"What kind of songs do you sing?"

"You know, all kinds of songs, for the morning and the evening, and for all the trees and the animals and the flowers. Now, for example, I could sing a pretty song about a young girl coming out of the woods and taking the harvesters their dinner."

"Could you really? Then go ahead and sing it!"

"Yes, but what's your name?"

"Brigitte."

Then I sang a song about the beautiful Brigitte in her straw hat and what she had in her basket, and how all the flowers stared at her, and the blue bindweed in the garden hedge reached out after her, and all the other particulars. She paid strict attention and said it was good. And when I told her I was hungry, she raised the lid of her basket and got out a piece of bread. I took a bite of it, continuing to walk rapidly, and she said: "You mustn't run while you're eating. One thing after the other." And so we sat down in the grass and I ate my bread, and she clasped her brown hands around her knees and looked at me.

"Will you sing something else for me?" she asked when I had finished.

"Of course I will. What shall it be?"

"About a girl whose darling ran away from her and she is sad."

"No, I can't do that. I don't know what that would be like, and anyway one oughtn't to be so sad. I must only sing bright, cheery songs, my father said. I'll sing to you about the cuckoo bird or the butterfly."

"Then you know nothing at all about love?" she asked.

"About love? Oh, yes, I do. That is the most beautiful thing of all."

I began at once and sang about the sunbeam that has fallen in love with the red poppy blossoms and how it sports with them and is filled with joy. And about the female finch when she is waiting for the male, and when he comes she flies away and pretends to be terrified. I sang further about the girl with brown eyes and about the youth who comes along and sings and is rewarded with a piece of bread; but now he does not want any more bread, he wants a kiss from the girl and wants to look into her brown eyes, and he will go on singing and will not stop until she begins to smile and shuts his mouth with her lips.

Then Brigitte bent over and shut my mouth with her lips and closed her eyes and then opened them again, and I looked into the close-up, brown-golden stars in which I saw myself and a few white meadow flowers reflected.

"The world is very beautiful," I said. "My father was quite right. Now I will help you carry your basket and we will take it to your people."

I picked up her basket and we walked on, her footsteps ringing with mine and her merriment matching my own, and the forest whispered gently and coolly from the mountain heights; I had never wandered with so much joy, I continued to sing gaily for a while until I had to stop from sheer superabundance: there were just too many songs coming from valley and mountain, from grass and trees and river and underbrush, all the whisperings and the stories.

Then I had to reflect: If I could simultaneously understand and sing all these thousands of songs of the world, about the grass and flowers and people and clouds and about everything, the leafy forests and the pine forests and all the animals, and also about the distant seas and mountains and the stars and the moon, and if all this could resound and sing inside me at once, then I would be God Almighty and each new song would take its place in the sky as a star.

But while I was thinking this, perfectly still inside, filled with wonder because such a thing had never come into my mind before, Brigitte stopped and held me back by the handle of the basket.

"Now I must go up this way," she said. "Our people are up there in the field. And you, where are you going? Will you come with me?"

"No, I cannot come with you. I must go out into the world. My best thanks for the bread, Brigitte, and for the kiss. I will think of you."

She took her dinner basket, and across it she once more bent her eyes upon me in the brown shadow, and her lips clung to mine and her kiss was so sweet and good that I almost grew sad from sheer gladness. Then I hastily called farewell and walked quickly off down the road.

The girl climbed slowly up the mountainside, and under the hanging foliage of the beech trees at the forest's edge she stopped and gazed after me, and when I signaled to her, waving my hat over my head, she nodded once and disappeared into the shadow of the beeches, as silent as a picture.

I, however, went on my way absorbed in my own thoughts until the road turned a corner.

There stood a mill and beside the mill a boat lay in the water and in it sat a solitary man who seemed to have been waiting just for me, for as I touched my hat to him and climbed aboard, the boat immediately began to move and ran downstream. I sat amidships and the man sat in the stern at the helm, and when I asked him where we were going he raised his head and stared at me with veiled gray eyes.

"Wherever you like," he said in a low tone. "Downstream and into the ocean, or to the great cities, you have your choice. It all belongs to me."

"It all belongs to you? Then you are the King?"

"Perhaps," he said. "And you are a poet, it seems. Then sing me a song as we travel."

I pulled myself together. Fear filled me because of the solemn gray man and because our boat moved so fast and silently down the river. I sang about the river, which carries boats and mirrors the sun and boils up on the rocky shores and is happy when it completes its wanderings.

The man's face remained expressionless, and when I stopped singing he nodded as silent as a dreamer, and then all at once to my astonishment he began to sing himself, and he too sang of the river and of the river's journey through the valleys, and his song was more beautiful and more powerful than mine, but in it everything sounded quite different.

The river, as he sang of it, rushed down from the hills like a roistering vandal, dark and wild; with gnashing teeth it fought against the constraint of mills and arching bridges; it loathed every boat it had to carry, and in its waves and long green waterweed it smilingly cradled the white corpses of the drowned.

All this pleased me not at all, and yet the sound of it was so beautiful and mysterious that I became wholly confused and fell silent in my distress. If what this subtle, clever old bard was singing in his muted voice was true, then all my songs were only nonsense and silly child's play. Then the world at bottom was not good and bright like God's own heart, but dark and desperate, evil and somber, and when the woods rustled, it was not from joy but from pain.

We voyaged on and the shadows lengthened, and each time I began to sing, it sounded less assured and my voice grew fainter, and each time the strange singer would answer me with a song that made the world ever more enigmatic and sorrowful and me ever more oppressed and sad.

My soul ached and I lamented not having stayed on shore with the flowers or with beautiful Brigitte, and to console myself in the growing dusk I began to sing again in a loud voice and I sang amid the red glow of evening the song of Brigitte and her kisses.

Then twilight came and I fell silent, and the man at the helm sang, and he too sang of love and the pleasures of love, of brown eyes and of blue eyes, of moist red lips, and his impassioned singing above the darkling flood was beautiful and moving, but in his song love too had become dark and terrifying and a deadly mystery for which men groped, mad and bleeding in their misery, and with which they tortured and killed one another.

I gave ear and grew as weary and troubled as though I had already been underway for years and had traveled through nothing but sorrow and misery. I felt a constant faint chilly stream of sorrow and anguish creeping across to me from the stranger, and into my heart.

"Well then, life is not the highest and best," I cried at last, bitterly, "but death is. Then I beseech you, sorrowful King, sing me a song of death!"

The man at the helm now sang about death, and his singing was more beautiful than anything I had ever heard. But even death was not the highest and best, even in death there was no comfort. Death was life, and life was death, and they were locked together in an eternal, mad love-battle, and this was the final word and the meaning of the world, and thence came a radiance that could glorify all misery, and thence came a shadow that troubled all joy and beauty and shrouded them in darkness. But from out of this darkness, joy burned more intimately and more beautifully, and love had a deeper glow within this night.

I listened, and had become perfectly still; there was no more will in me save that of this strange man. His glance rested on me calmly and with a certain sad kindliness, and his gray eyes were full of the sorrow and the beauty of the world. He smiled at me and then I took heart and pleaded in my misery: "Oh, let us put about, you! I am fearful here in the dark and I want to turn back and go where I can find Brigitte, or home to my father."

The man stood up and pointed into the night, and the lantern shone bright on his thin, determined face. "There is no way back," he said solemnly and gently. "One must continue to go forward if one wants to fathom the world. And you have already had what is best and finest from the girl with the brown eyes, and the farther you are from her the better and finer it will be. But no matter, sail on, wherever you wish. I will give you my place at the helm!"

I was in deathly despair and yet I saw that he was right. Full of yearning, I thought of Brigitte and of my home and of everything that had so recently been near and bright and my own, and that I had now lost. But now I must take the stranger's place and man the helm, so it must be.

Therefore, I got up in silence and stepped through the boat toward the pilot's seat, and the man came toward me silently, and as we were passing he looked fixedly into my face and handed me his lantern.

But when I was seated at the helm and had placed the lantern beside me, I was alone in the boat. I recognized with a deep shudder that the man had disappeared, and yet I was not surprised, I had had a premonition. It seemed to me that the beautiful day of wandering and Brigitte and my father and my homeland had been only dreams and that I was old and sorrowful and had already been voyaging forever and ever on this nocturnal river.

I knew that I must not call the man, and recognition of the truth came over me like a chill.

To make sure of what I already suspected, I leaned out over the water and lifted the lantern, and out of the black watery mirror a face peered up at me, a face with severe and solemn features and gray eyes, an old knowing face, and it was I.

And since no way led back, I voyaged forth over the dark waters deeper into the night.

Strange News
from Another Star

A SOUTHERN PROVINCE of our lovely star had suffered a great calamity. An earthquake accompanied by fearful thunderstorms and floods had destroyed three large villages together with all the farms and gardens, fields and woods. A great many people and animals had been killed and, saddest of all, there was a total lack of flowers in adequate quantity to wreathe the dead and appropriately adorn their last resting places.

Whatever could be done was, of course, done promptly. Immediately after the dreadful hour, messengers bearing an urgent appeal in the name of charity hurried through the nearby countryside, and from all the towers in the province precentors intoned the deeply moving verses known from of old as the Hymn to the Goddess of Compassion, whose strains no man could resist. Sympathizers and helpers came in throngs from all the cities and towns, and the unfortunates who were shelterless were showered with cordial invitations from relations, friends, and even strangers, to share their homes. Food and clothing, horses and wagons, tools, stone, and wood, and many other materials were brought in from all sides, and while the old men, women, and children were led away by kindly hands, were comforted and cared for, while the injured were conscientiously washed and bandaged and a search for the dead was carried out among the ruins, other people were already at work clearing away fallen roofs, propping up sagging walls with beams, and preparing for a swift rebuilding. At first a breath of horror lingered in the air and there emanated from all the dead a reminder of grief and admonition to reverent silence, but soon there came into every countenance and voice a more cheerful air, a certain muted festiveness: for the common effort in this urgent undertaking and the very fact of doing something so handsome and so deserving of thanks reassured every heart. Whereas the rescuers had begun their work in awe and silence, shortly a happy voice could be heard here and there, a subdued song accompanying the shared labor, and, as might be expected, of all the things sung the favorites were the two ancient proverbs: "How blessed to bring aid to one newly afflicted; his heart drinks up kindness as a parched garden drinks up spring rain and responds with flowers and thanksgiving." And that other: "The serenity of God flows forth from action partaken of in common."

But now they were confronted by that lamentable lack of flowers. To be sure, the dead that had been found first had been adorned with the flowers and boughs that had been collected from the ruined gardens. Then people had fetched all the available flowers from nearby towns. But the great misfortune was that the three ruined communities had had the largest and finest gardens of flowers of that season of the year. People had visited them annually to see the narcissus and crocuses, which were not to be found elsewhere in such immense quantities or so carefully cultivated or of such marvelously colored varieties. And all this was now ruined and gone. And so people stood about in bewilderment, not knowing how the requirements of tradition were to be met for all these dead, the tradition that every human being and animal must be adorned at death with the flowers of the season and that interment be all the richer and more magnificent the more sudden and tragic the manner of death.

The Eldest of the Province, who had arrived in one of the first rescue vehicles, soon found himself so overwhelmed by questions, pleas, and complaints that he had trouble maintaining his calm cheerfulness. But with an effort he managed to quiet his heart, and his eyes remained bright and friendly, his voice clear and courteous, and his lips under his white beard never for an instant lost the peaceful, kindly smile that became him as a wise man and a counselor.

"My friends," he said, "a disaster has come upon us through the will of the gods, who desire to test us. We can rebuild and return to our brothers everything that has been destroyed here, and I am grateful to the gods that I at a great age have been allowed to witness the way you have all come hither, leaving your own affairs, to help our brothers. But where will we find the flowers to adorn these dead beautifully and properly to celebrate their transformation? For so long as we are alive and present, it must not happen that a single one of these weary pilgrims is interred without the proper floral offering. I do not doubt that you agree."

"Yes," they all cried, "that is our opinion too."

"I knew it," the Eldest said in his fatherly voice. "Now I shall tell you what we must do, my friends. We must transport all these weary ones whom we cannot bury today to the great summer temple high in the mountains where there is still snow. There they will be safe and will remain unchanged until their flowers can be procured. But there is only one who can help us obtain so many flowers at this season. Only the King can do that. Therefore, one of us must be sent to the King to sue for his help."

And once more they all nodded and cried: "Yes, yes, to the King!"

"So be it," the Eldest said, and everyone was happy to see the radiant smile under his white beard. "But whom shall we send to the King? He must be young and vigorous, for the journey is long, and we must provide him with our best horse. However, he must also be handsome and pure of heart and bright of eye so that the King's heart will be unable to resist him. He need not say much, but his eyes must know how to speak. No doubt the best thing would be to send a child, the handsomest boy in our community, but how could he make such a trip? You must help me, my friends, and if there is anyone here who is willing to undertake this mission or who knows a suitable person, I beg him to speak up."

The Eldest fell silent, glancing about with his bright eyes, but no one stepped forward and no voice was raised.

When he had repeated his question a second and then a third time, there came out of the throng a sixteen-year-old youth who looked hardly more than a child. He cast his eyes to the ground and blushed as he saluted the Eldest.

The Eldest looked at him and saw in an instant that this was the proper messenger. However, he smiled and said: "It is fine that you wish to be our messenger, but how comes it that of all this crowd you are the one to volunteer?"

Then the youth raised his eyes to the ancient man and said: "If there is no other here who wishes to go, then let me go."

But a man in the crowd shouted: "Send him, Eldest. We know him. He comes from this village and the earthquakes destroyed his flower garden. It was the most beautiful flower garden in our town."

The Eldest looked in kindly fashion into the boy's eyes and asked: "Are you so grieved about your flowers?"

The youth answered very softly: "I am grieved, but it is not on that account that I have volunteered. I had a dear friend and also a beautiful favorite colt, they both were killed in the earthquake and now they are lying in our hall and there must be flowers so that they can be buried."

The Eldest blessed him by the laying on of hands, and very quickly the best horse was chosen for him and he sprang instantly to the horse's back, tapped him on the neck and nodded goodbye, then he galloped out of the village, straight across the wet, devastated fields and away.

The youth rode all day. To reach the capital and the King as quickly as he could, he chose the way over the mountains, and at evening as it was growing dark he was leading his steed by the reins up a steep path amid woods and rocks.

A huge dark bird such as he had never seen before flew in front of him, and he followed it until the bird alighted on the roof of a little open temple. The youth left his horse in a forest glade and strode through the wooden pillars into the simple sanctuary. As sacrificial stone he found only a boulder set up, a block of black stone of a kind not to be found in that neighborhood, and on it the strange symbol of a deity unknown to the messenger: a heart being devoured by a bird of prey.

To show his reverence to the godhead, he offered as a gift a blue bellflower he had plucked at the foot of the mountain and thrust into his buttonhole. Thereupon he lay down in a corner, for he was very weary and wished to sleep.

But he could not find sleep, which customarily stood each night by his bed. The bellflower on the rock or the black stone itself, or whatever it might be, exuded a penetrating, strange, disturbing scent, the uncanny symbol of the god shone with a spectral radiance in the dark hall, and on the roof the strange bird sat and from time to time beat its enormous wings so that there was a rustling in the trees like a coming storm.

Thus it came about that in the middle of the night the young man got up and walked out of the temple and looked up at the bird. The latter beat its wings and stared at the youth.

"Why are you not asleep?" asked the bird.

"I do not know," the youth said. "Perhaps because I have learned about sorrow."

"Just what kind of sorrow?"

"My friend and my favorite steed both have perished."

"Is dying so bad, then?" the bird asked disdainfully.

"Oh no, great bird, it is not so bad, it is only a farewell, but that is not the reason I am sad. The bad thing is that we cannot bury my friend and my beautiful horse because we have no more flowers."

"There are worse things than that," the bird said, and rustled its feathers impatiently.

"No, bird, there is certainly nothing worse. Whoever is buried without floral offering is debarred from rebirth in accordance with his heart's desire. And whoever buries his dead without celebrating the floral festival will see the shades of his departed in his dreams. You can see how it is; even now I cannot sleep because my dead are still without flowers."

The bird emitted a rasping screech from its hooked beak.

"Young man, you are ignorant of sorrow if you have learned nothing beyond this. Have you never heard tell of the great evils? Of hatred, murder, and jealousy?"

When he heard these words spoken, the youth felt as though he were dreaming. Then he bethought himself and said humbly: "To be sure, O bird, I remember: these things are written about in the old histories and legends. But surely that is outside reality, or perhaps it was that way in the world once a long time ago before there were any flowers or any kindly gods. Who wants to think of it!"

The bird laughed softly. Then it stretched itself taller and said to the boy in its harsh voice: "So now you want to go to the King, and shall I show you the way?"

"Oh, you know the way," the youth cried happily. "Yes, if you're willing, please do."

Then the great bird glided silently to the ground, noiselessly spread its wings apart, and directed the youth to leave his horse behind and come with it to the King.

The messenger seated himself and rode on the bird. "Shut your eyes!" the bird commanded, and the young man did so, and they flew through the darkness of the sky as silently and softly as the flight of an owl, only the cold air whistled around the messenger's ears. And they flew and flew all night long.

When it was early morning they stopped, and the bird cried: "Open your eyes," and the youth opened his eyes. He found himself standing at the edge of a forest, and beneath him in the first glow of morning lay a glittering plain, so bright that it dazzled him.

"You will find me here at the edge of the forest again," the bird cried. It shot into the sky like an arrow and immediately disappeared in the blue.

A strange feeling came over the young messenger as he wandered out of the forest into the broad plain. Everything round about him was so different that he did not know whether he was awake or dreaming. There were meadows and trees like the ones at home, the sun was shining, and the wind played in the tall grass, but there were no people or animals, no dwellings or gardens; instead, it seemed as though an earthquake had occurred here exactly as in the youth's homeland; ruins of buildings, broken branches and uprooted trees, twisted fences and abandoned farming implements were strewn about, and suddenly he saw lying in the middle of a field a dead man in a horrible state of decomposition. The youth felt revulsion and a touch of nausea rose in his throat, for he had never before seen such a thing. Not even the dead man's face had been covered and it was already ravaged by birds and by decay; the youth gathered leaves and a few flowers and, with averted eyes, covered the dead countenance.

An inexpressibly horrible and oppressive smell hung warm and inescapable over the whole plain. Another corpse lay near at hand in the grass encircled by a flock of ravens, and a horse without a head, and bones of men or animals, and all had been left exposed to the sun, no one seemed to have thought of floral offerings and burial. The youth began to fear that an incredible disaster must have killed each and every person in this land; there were so many dead that he had to give up picking flowers to cover their faces. Full of dread, his eyes half closed, he wandered on, and there poured in upon him from all sides carrion stench and the smell of blood, and from a thousand piles of ruins and heaps of dead there welled mightier and mightier waves of unspeakable misery and sorrow. The messenger believed he had been caught in a terrifying dream that was an admonition from the Heavenly Ones because his own dead were still without floral offerings and without burial. Then he remembered what the mysterious bird on the temple roof had said the night before, and he seemed once more to hear the harsh voice asserting: "There are many worse things."

Now he realized that the bird had brought him to another star and that everything his eyes saw was real and true. He recalled the feeling with which sometimes as a boy he had listened to frightening tales of primeval times. This special feeling he now experienced again: a shuddering horror, and behind the horror a quiet, happy assurance in his heart, for all this was infinitely remote and long past. Here everything was like a horror story, this whole strange world of outrage, corpses, and carrion birds seemed without sense and without control, subject to incomprehensible laws, mad laws according to which the evil, the absurd, and the ugly always triumphed instead of the beautiful and good.

And then he caught sight of a living man walking across the field, a farmer or a farm hand, and he ran quickly toward him and called out. As the youth drew near, he was startled and his heart was filled with compassion, for this farmer looked frighteningly ugly and hardly at all like a child of the sun. He appeared to be a selfish and disgruntled man, a man accustomed to seeing only what was false and ugly and evil, one who lived constantly in horrifying nightmares. In his eyes and in his whole face and being, there was no trace of serenity or kindness, no glimmer of graciousness and trust, these simplest and most natural of virtues seemed absent in this unfortunate.

But the youth pulled himself together and with great friendliness approached the fellow as one distinguished by misfortune, greeted him in brotherly fashion, and spoke to him with a smile. The ugly one stood as though turned to stone, looking with amazement out of great troubled eyes. His voice, when he spoke, was harsh and unmusical like the bellowing of cattle; nevertheless, he could not resist the serenity and undemanding trustfulness in the youth's eyes. And when he had stared for a while at the stranger, there broke over his rude and tormented face a kind of smile or grin—ugly enough but gentle and amazed, like the first faint smile of a soul reborn that has just emerged from the lowest regions of the earth.

"What do you want of me?" he asked.

In accordance with the custom of his homeland, the youth replied: "I thank you, friend, and I beg you to tell me whether there is any service I can do for you."

When the farmer was silent, smiling in astonishment and embarrassment, the messenger said to him: "Tell me, friend, what has happened here? What is this dreadful and horrifying thing?" And he gestured round about with his hand.

The farmer had trouble understanding, and when the messenger had repeated his question, he said: "Have you never seen this before? This is war, this is a battlefield." He pointed to a pile of blackened ruins and cried: "That was my house," and when the stranger looked with heartfelt sympathy into the farmer's impure eyes, he lowered them and stared at the ground.

"Haven't you a king?" the youth went on to ask, and when the farmer said they had, he asked further: "Then where is he?" The fellow pointed toward an encampment that was just visible, remote and tiny in the distance. The messenger said farewell, placing his hand on the man's forehead, and departed. The farmer, however, raised both hands to his forehead, shook his heavy head in perplexity, and stood for a time staring after the stranger.

The latter ran and ran, past ruins and horrors, until he came to the encampment. There were armed men everywhere, standing or hurrying about; no one seemed to notice him, and he walked between the men and tents until he came to the biggest and handsomest tent in the camp, which was the King's tent. He entered.

Inside, the King was sitting on a simple, low couch, his mantle beside him, and behind him in deeper shadow crouched a servant who had fallen asleep. The King sat bowed over, deep in thought. His face was beautiful and sad, a shock of gray hair hung over his sun-tanned forehead, his sword lay in front of him on the ground. The youth greeted him with deep reverence, as he would have greeted his own King, and he stood waiting with arms crossed on his breast until the King caught sight of him.

"Who are you?" the King asked severely, drawing his dark brows together, but his glance clung to the pure calm features of the stranger, and the youth looked at him so trustingly and so intimately that the King's voice grew milder.

"I have seen you somewhere before," he said meditatively, "or you look like someone I knew in my childhood."

"I am a stranger," said the messenger.

"Then it was a dream," the King said softly. "You remind me of my mother. Speak to me. Explain."

The youth began: "A bird brought me here. In my country there was an earthquake and so we wanted to bury our dead and there were no flowers."

"No flowers?" said the King.

"No, no more flowers at all. And it is an ill thing, is it not, if one has to bury a dead man and cannot celebrate a flower festival for him; for after all he must enter into his transformation with splendor and joy."

Then suddenly the messenger remembered how many unburied dead lay out there on that horrible field, and he stopped speaking, and the King looked at him and nodded and sighed heavily.

"I was on my way to our King to ask him for many flowers," the messenger continued. "But when I was in the temple in the mountains, a great bird came and said that he would take me to the King, and he brought me through the air to you. O dear King, it was the temple of an unknown deity on whose roof the bird sat and there was a very strange symbol on the altar of this god: a heart being devoured by a bird of prey. But during the night I had a conversation with that great bird and now for the first time I can understand his words, for he said that there was much, much more suffering and evil in the world than I knew. And now I am here, and I have crossed that huge field, and during these hours I have seen infinite suffering and misfortune—oh, much more than our most horrible tales contain. Now I have come to you, O King, and I would like to ask you whether I can be of any service to you."

The King, who had listened with attention, tried to smile, but his beautiful face was so sad and embittered that he could not smile.

"I thank you," he said. "You cannot do me any service. But you have put me in mind of my mother, and for that I thank you."

The youth was troubled because the King could not smile. "You are so sad," he said to him. "Is it because of this war?"

"Yes," said the King.

The youth could not help breaking a rule of courtesy toward this heavily burdened and yet, as he felt, noble man by asking: "But tell me, I beseech you, why do you carry on such wars on your star? Who is to blame for them? Are you yourself in part responsible?"

The King seemed angered at this audacity and for a time stared at the messenger. But he could not continue to meet with his dark gaze the bright and guileless eyes of the stranger.

"You are a child," said the King, "and there are things you cannot understand. War is no one's fault, it occurs of itself, like storm and lightning, and all of us who have to fight wars, we are not their originators, we are only their victims."

"Then no doubt you die very easily?" the youth asked. "With us at home, to be sure, death is not greatly feared, and most people approach the transformation willingly and happily; but never would anyone dare to kill another. On your star it must be different."

The King shook his head. "It is true that killing is not rare among us," he said, "but we consider it the worst of crimes. Only in war is it allowed because in war no one kills for his own advantage, out of hatred or envy, but all do only what society demands of them. You are mistaken, however, if you believe that we die easily. If you look into the faces of our dead, you will see. They die hard, they die hard and unreconciled."

The youth listened to all this in astonishment at the madness and difficulty of the people's way of life on this star. He would have liked to ask many more questions, but he knew with certainty that he would never understand the whole context of these dark and terrifying things; indeed, he felt no real wish to understand them. Either these pitiable creatures belonged to a lower order, were still without the bright gods and were ruled by demons, or some unique mischance, some horrid error, prevailed on this star. And it seemed to him altogether too painful and cruel to go on questioning this king, compelling him to answers and confessions which could only be bitterly humiliating. These people who lived in the dark dread of death and yet slew one another in masses, whose faces were composed with such ignoble coarseness as that of the farmer or with such deep and terrible sorrow as that of the King, they caused him pain, and yet in their disturbing and shaming fashion they seemed to him so strange as to be almost laughable, laughable and silly.

But there was one question he could not repress. If these poor souls were retarded beings, belated children, sons of a latter-day outcast star, if their lives passed like a convulsive shudder and ended in slaughter, if they left their dead lying in the fields, or even perhaps ate them—for there had been talk of that in some of those horror stories of primeval times—then nevertheless there must be some intimation of the future, a dream of the gods, something like the seed of soul latent in them; otherwise, this whole unbeautiful world would indeed be but a meaningless error.

"Forgive me, King," the youth said ingratiatingly, "forgive me if I put one more question to you before leaving your astounding country."

"Go ahead and ask," the King said, for to him this stranger seemed a paradox, in many ways he seemed a cultivated, mature, and incredibly enlightened spirit, but in others like a small child whom one must spare and not take quite seriously.

"O stranger King," the messenger now said, "you have made me sad. Behold, I come from another country, and the great bird on the temple roof was right: here with you there is infinitely more misery than I could ever have imagined; a dream of terror, so your life seems to me, and I do not know whether you are ruled by gods or demons. Behold, O King, with us there is a legend, and until now I have considered it mythical nonsense, empty smoke, it is the legend that once with us too there were such things as war and murder and despair. These terrifying words which have long been unknown in our language are to be found in the old storybooks and to us they sound horrible and also a little ridiculous. Today I have learned that they are all true, and I see you and your people doing and suffering things that I knew only from the dreadful tales of antiquity. But now tell me: have you not in your souls an intimation that you are not doing what is right? Have you not a longing for bright, serene gods, for understanding, for cheerful leaders and mentors? At night do you never dream of a different and more beautiful life in which no one wants anything save for the common good? Where reason and order prevail, where people always meet one another with cheerfulness and consideration? Have you never had the thought that the world might be a single whole and that it might be beneficent and healing to rely on this presentiment and reverence the whole and serve it with love? Do you know nothing of what we at home call music, and the service of God, and blessedness?"

As he listened to these words, the King had bowed his head. Now he raised it, and his face had changed, it shone with the faint shimmer of a smile and tears stood in his eyes.

"Beautiful boy," said the King, "I do not rightly know whether you are a child or a wise man or perhaps an immortal. But I can tell you that we harbor within our souls all those things of which you speak. We have a presentiment of happiness, of freedom, of the gods. We have a legend about a wise man of long ago who perceived the unity of the world as the harmonious music of the heavenly spheres. Does that answer you? Look you, perhaps you are a saint from the beyond, or you may even be God himself, even so there is no happiness in your heart, no power, no will of which there is not a presentiment, a reflection, a remote shadow in our hearts too."

And suddenly he drew himself up to his full height, and the youth stood amazed, for the King's face for a moment was bathed in a bright, unshadowed smile like the glow of morning.

"Go now," he cried to the messenger, "go now and leave us to our wars and our murders! You have made my heart soft, you have put me in mind of my mother, enough, enough of this, dear beautiful boy. Go now, flee before the next battle begins! I shall think of you when blood flows and cities burn, and I will think of the world as a whole from which even our blindness and our rage and our ruthlessness cannot cut us off. Farewell, and give my greetings to your star and my greetings to that deity whose symbol is a heart being devoured by a bird! I know so well that heart and that bird. And note this, my beautiful friend from afar: when you think of your friend, when you think of the poor King embroiled in war, do not think of him sitting on his couch plunged in misery, but rather think of him as he stood with tears in his eyes and blood on his hands and smiled!"

The King raised the flap of the tent with his own hand, not waking his servant, and let the stranger depart. The youth, plunged in new thoughts, hurried back across the plain, and in the evening sunshine he saw on the horizon a great city in flames, and he made his way over dead men and the rotting carcasses of horses until it was dark and he had reached the edge of the forest.

There the great bird was already descending from the clouds, it took him on its wings and flew back through the night as silently and softly as the flight of an owl.

When the youth awoke from an unquiet sleep, he was lying in the little temple in the mountains, and before the temple in the wet grass stood his horse, whinnying at the dawn. But about the great bird and about his journey to another star, about the King and about the battlefield, he no longer remembered anything at all. All that remained was a shadow in his soul, a little obscure pain as from a small thorn, the way helpless sympathy hurts, and a little unsatisfied wish such as sometimes torments us in dreams until finally we encounter the person to whom we secretly long to show our love, whose joy we secretly long to share, whose smile we secretly long to see.

The messenger mounted his horse and rode all day long and came to the capital and into the presence of his King, and he proved to be the right messenger. For the King received him with the greeting of grace by touching his forehead and exclaiming: "Your eyes have spoken to my heart, and my heart has assented. Your request is granted before I have so much as heard it."

Forthwith the messenger received a charter from the King proclaiming that all the flowers of the whole country were at his disposal, and companions and outriders and servants joined him, and horses and wagons appeared, and when after a few days he made his way around the mountains, returning home on the level highway to his province and his town, he was accompanied by wagons and carts and hampers, horses and donkeys, all bearing the most beautiful flowers from the gardens and hothouses of the north, and there were enough flowers to wreathe the bodies of the dead and richly adorn their graves as well as to plant as memorial on each grave a flower, a bush, and a young fruit tree, as custom demands. And the pain for his friend and his favorite horse left him and was replaced by a tranquil, happy memory when he had adorned them too and buried them and over their graves had planted two flowers, two bushes, and two fruit trees.

After he had thus performed his duties and assuaged his heart, the memory of that journey through the night began to stir in his mind, and he besought those closest to him for a day of solitude, and sat under the meditation tree for a day and a night, and spread out in thought, clear and unwrinkled, the pictures of what had happened to him on that alien star. As a result he approached the Eldest one day, begged him for a private conversation, and told him all.

The Eldest gave ear, sat plunged in thought, and finally asked: "My friend, did you see all this with your eyes or was it a dream?"

"I do not know," said the youth. "I believe in fact that it may have been a dream. However, with your indulgence, may it be said there seems hardly any difference if these happenings were presented in actuality to my senses. A shadow of sadness has remained within me, and in the midst of joy in life a chilling wind blows upon me from that distant star. Therefore, I ask you, reverend sir, what shall I do?"

"Tomorrow go again to the mountains," said the Eldest, "and to the place where you found the temple. The symbol of that god of whom I have never heard seems strange to me, and it may well be that he is a god from another star. On the other hand, perhaps that temple and its god are so old that they belong to the times of our earliest forebears, to those long-ago days when it is said there were still weapons, horror, and the fear of death among us. Go to that temple, my friend, and make an offering there of flowers, honey, and song."

The youth spoke his thanks and followed the directions of the Eldest. He took a bowl of fine honey such as is set before the guests of honor at the first Festival of the Bees in early summer, and he carried his lute with him. In the mountains he found the place where he had once picked the blue bellflower, and he found the steep rocky mountain path through the woods where he had led his horse. But he could not again discover the place of the temple or the temple itself, or the black sacrificial stone, the wooden columns, the roof or the great bird on the roof, not that day and not the next day, and no one could tell him of any such temple as he described.

So he turned back toward home and when he came to the Sanctuary of Loving Remembrance, he went in and offered up the honey, sang a song to the accompaniment of his lute, and commended to the Deity of Loving Remembrance the dream he had had, the temple and the bird, the poor farmer, the dead on the battlefield, and most especially the King in his war tent. Thereafter, he went home lightened in heart, hung up on the wall of his room the symbol of the unity of the worlds, recuperated in deep sleep from the experiences of the past days, and next morning began to help his neighbors, who were busy in garden and field eradicating the last traces of the earthquake, singing as they worked.

The Hard Passage

BESIDE THE DARK OPENING in the cliff at the entrance to the gorge I stood hesitating, and turned to look back.

The sun was shining in that pleasant green world, above the meadows brownish grass blossoms waved and flickered. It was good to be out there in warmth and well-loved ease, out where one's soul hummed deep and satisfied like a hairy bumblebee in the heavy fragrance and light; perhaps I was a fool to want to leave all this and climb up into the mountain range.

My guide touched me gently on the arm. I tore my eyes away from the beloved landscape, the way a man forcibly frees himself from a warm bath. Now I saw the gorge lying in sunless darkness, a little black stream crept out of the cleft, pale grass grew in small tufts on its bank, in its bed lay stones that it had tumbled there, stones of all shades, pale and dead like the bones of creatures that had died long ago.

"We'll take a rest," I said to the guide.

He smiled indulgently, and we sat down. It was cool, and out of the rocky entrance flowed a gentle stream of dark, stone-cold air.

Nasty, nasty to go this way! Nasty to force oneself through this cheerless rocky entrance, to stride across this cold brook, to climb up in darkness into this narrow ragged gorge!

"The way looks horrible," I said in hesitation.

As though from the dying embers of a fire, a strong unbelievable unreasoning hope flared up within me, the hope that we could perhaps still turn back, that my guide might even now allow himself to be persuaded, that we might be spared all this. Yes, why not, really? Wasn't it a thousand times more beautiful in the place we had just left? Did not life there flow richer, warmer, more enchanting? And wasn't I a human being, a childlike, short-lived creature with a right to some share of happiness, to a cozy corner in the sun, to the sight of blue sky and flowers?

No, I wanted to stay where I was. I had no wish to play the hero and martyr! I would be content all my life if I were allowed to stay in the valley and in the sun.

Already I was beginning to shiver; it was impossible to linger here for long.

"You're shivering," said the guide. "We had better move on."

Thereupon he stood up and for a moment stretched to his full height and looked down at me with a smile; there was neither derision nor sympathy in the smile, neither harshness nor compassion. There was nothing there but understanding, nothing but knowledge. That smile said: "I know you. I know your fear and how you feel, and I have by no means forgotten your boastings of yesterday and the day before. Every rabbity dodge of cowardice your soul is now indulging in, every flirtatious glance at the lovely sunshine out there is well known and familiar to me before you act it out."

With this smile the guide looked at me and took the first stride into the dark rocky chasm ahead of us, and I hated him and loved him as a condemned man hates and loves the ax above his neck. Above all, I hated and despised his knowledge, his leadership and calmness, his lack of amiable weaknesses, and I hated everything in myself that agreed with him, that approved him, that wanted to be like him and to follow him.

Already he had taken a number of steps, walking on the stones through the black brook, and was just on the point of disappearing from sight around the first bend.

"Stop!" I cried, so full of fear that I was compelled to think at the same time: If this were a dream, then at this very moment my terror would dissolve it and I would wake up. "Stop!" I cried. "I cannot do it, I am not yet ready."

The guide stopped and looked across at me in silence, without reproach, but with that dreadful understanding of his, with that unbearable knowledge and presentiment, that having-completely-understood-in-advance.

"Would you rather that we turn back?" he asked, and he had not finished saying the last word when I knew, full of rebellion, that I would say no, that I would have to say no. And at the same time, everything long familiar, loved, and trusted within me cried in desperation: "Say yes, say yes!" and the whole world and my homeland were chained like an iron ball to my leg.

I wanted to shout yes, though I knew very well that I could not do it.

Then with outstretched arm the guide pointed back into the valley, and I turned around once more toward that well-loved region. And now what I saw was the most painful thing that could have happened to me: I saw my beloved valleys and fields lying pale and lusterless under a white enfeebled sun, the colors clashed, false and shrill, the shadows were a rusty black and without magic, and the heart had been cut out of everything, everything, the charm and fragrance were gone—everything smelled and tasted of things long since over-indulged in to the point of nausea. Oh, how well I knew all this, how I feared and hated this horrid trick of the guide, this degradation of what was dear and pleasant to me, causing the sap and spirit to drain out of it, falsifying the smells and secretly poisoning the colors! Oh, I knew this; what was wine but yesterday, today was vinegar. And the vinegar would never become wine again. Never again.

I was silent and sad as I followed the guide. He was, of course, right, now as always. It was a good thing at least that he remained visibly with me instead—as so often happened at moments of decision—of disappearing suddenly and leaving me alone, alone with that alien voice inside my breast into which at such times he transformed himself.

I was silent, but my heart cried passionately: "Only stay, I will assuredly follow!"

The stones in the brook were horribly slippery; it was tiring and dizzying to walk like this, step by step on nar-

row wet stones that slipped away and shrank under one's
feet. At the same time the path in the brook began to rise
steeply and the dark cliff walls drew closer together, they
swelled ominously and every corner showed the malicious
intention of clamping down behind us and cutting off our
retreat forever. Over wart-covered yellow rocks ran a vis-
cous slimy sheet of water. No sky above our heads, neither
clouds nor blue.

I walked and walked, following my guide and often
closing my eyes in fear and disgust. Then there was a dark
flower growing beside the path, velvety black with an air
of sadness. It was beautiful and spoke to me familiarly,
but my guide walked faster and I felt that if I lingered for
a single moment, if I bestowed so much as one more
glance on that sad, velvety eye, then my depression and
hopeless gloom would become overwhelming and unen-
durable, and my spirit would remain forever imprisoned
in that mocking region of senselessness and madness.

Wet and dirty, I crept on, and as the damp walls came
closer together above us my guide began to sing his old
chant of consolation. In his strong clear youthful voice he
sang in time to each stride: "I will, I will, I will!" I knew
very well that he wanted to encourage me and spur me on,
he wanted to divert me from the hideous toil and hope-
lessness of this hellish journey. I knew that he was waiting for me to chime in with his singsong. But I refused to
do it, I would not grant him that victory. Was I in any
mood to sing? And wasn't I a human being, a poor simple
fellow who in defiance of his own heart had been drawn
into situations and deeds which God could not expect of

him? Were not every forget-me-not and every pink allowed to stay where they had grown along the brook, to bloom and wither after their own fashion?

"I will, I will, I will!" the guide sang uninterruptedly. Oh, if only I had been able to turn back! But with my guide's skillful help I had long since clambered over walls and abysses across which there was no possible return. Tears burned in my throat but I dared not weep, that least of all. And so defiantly and loudly I joined in the guide's song, in the same rhythm and tone but not with his words; instead I sang determinedly: "I must, I must, I must!" But it was not easy to sing and climb at the same time, soon I lost my breath and was forced to fall silent, gasping. But he went on singing unwearied: "I will, I will, I will," and in time he compelled me after all to join in singing his words. Now the climbing was easier and I no longer felt under compulsion, in fact I wished to go on, and as for weariness from singing, there was no further trace of that.

Then there was a brightness inside me and as this increased, the smooth cliff receded too, became drier, became kinder, often aided the slipping foot, and above all more and more of the clear blue heavens appeared, like a little blue stream between rocky banks, and soon like a little blue lake that grew longer and wider.

I tried to exert my will more intensely and more profoundly, and the heavenly lake continued to grow and the path became more practicable, yes, at times I hurried unencumbered over long stretches, easily keeping pace with my guide. And then unexpectedly I saw the summit close above us, steep and glittering in the shining sunny air.

A short distance below the summit we crawled out of the narrow crevasse, sun assailed my dazzled eyes, and when I opened them again my knees shook with dread, for I found myself standing free and without support on a sheer ridge; round about were infinite space and terrifying blue depths, only the narrow summit towered above us thin as a ladder. But sky and sun were there once more, and so we clambered up that last terrifying pitch as well, step by step, with compressed lips and knotted brows. And stood on the summit, trivial figures on the sun-warmed rock in the sharp, bitingly thin air.

That was a strange mountain and a strange summit! We had reached the top by climbing over completely naked walls of stone, and on that summit there grew out of the stone a tree, a sturdy squat tree with several short powerful branches. There it stood, inconceivably lonely and strange, hard and unyielding in the rock, with the cool blue of heaven between its branches. And at the top of this tree sat a black bird harshly singing.

Quiet dream of brief repose above the world, the sun blazed, the rock glowed, the tree rose unyielding, the bird sang harshly. Its harsh song signified: Eternity, Eternity! The black bird sang, and its blank hard eye stared at us like a black crystal. Hard to bear was its gaze, hard to bear its song, and frightful above all were the loneliness and emptiness of that place, the expanse of the barren heavens. To die was inconceivable bliss, to stay there nameless pain. Something must happen, at once, instantly; otherwise, we and the world would turn to stone from sheer horror. I felt the event wafted toward us hot and oppressive like a puff of wind before a storm. I felt it flickering over my body and soul like a burning fever. It threatened, it was coming, it was there.

—Suddenly the bird whirled from its bough, plunged headlong into space.

With a leap my guide dived into the blue, fell toward the flashing heavens, flew away.

Now the wave of fate had reached its peak, now it tore away my heart, now it broke in silence.

And already I was falling, I plunged, leaped, I flew; wrapped in a cold vortex, I shot, blissful and palpitating with ecstatic pain, down through infinity to the mother's breast.

A Dream Sequence

I T SEEMED to me that I had already spent a vast amount of turgid, unprofitable time in that stuffy salon through whose northern windows shone the false sea and the imitation fiords, and where nothing attracted or held my attention save the presence of the beautiful, suspect lady whom I took to be a sinner. In vain I longed to have just one good look at her face. That face floated dimly amid loose dark hair, a cloud of sweet pallor and nothing more. Possibly her eyes were dark brown, I felt some inner reason to expect that; but if so her eyes would not match the face I was trying to read into that indeterminate pallor, whose shape I knew lay buried in deep, inaccessible levels of my memory.

Finally something happened. The two young men entered. They greeted the lady with elaborate courtesy and were introduced to me. Monkeys, I thought, and was annoyed at myself because the pretty, stylish cut and fit of the reddish-brown jacket one of them was wearing filled me with shame and envy. A horrible feeling of envy toward the irreproachable, unabashed smiler! "Pull yourself together!" I commanded inwardly. The two young men reached indifferently for my extended hand—why had I offered it?—wearing derisive smiles.

Then I realized that something was wrong about me

and felt a disturbing chill creeping up my legs. I glanced down and grew pale on seeing that I stood in my stocking feet, shoeless. Again and again these shabby, miserable, sordid frustrations and disadvantages! It never happened to others that they appeared naked or half naked in salons before a company of the irreproachably correct! Disheartened, I tried at least to conceal my left foot with my right; as I did, my eyes strayed through the window and I saw the steep wild blue ocean cliffs threatening with false and sinister colors and demonic intent. Worried and seeking help, I looked at the two strangers, full of hatred for these people and full of a greater hatred for myself—nothing turned out right for me, that was the trouble. And why did I feel responsible for that stupid sea? Well, if that was the way I felt, then I *was* responsible. Beseechingly I looked the reddish-brown one in the face, his cheeks shone with health and careful grooming, and I knew perfectly well that I was exposing myself to no purpose, that he could not be influenced.

At that moment he noticed my feet in their coarse dark-green socks—oh, I could still be thankful there were no holes in them—and smiled disagreeably. He nudged his comrade and pointed at my feet. The other, too, grinned in derision.

"Just look at the sea!" I shouted, gesturing toward the window.

The man in the reddish-brown jacket shrugged his shoulders; it did not occur to him to so much as turn toward the window, and he said something to the other which I only half understood, but it was aimed at me and had to do with fellows in stocking feet who really ought not to be tolerated in such a salon. As I listened, the word "salon" again had for me, as it had in my childhood, the half-seductive, half-meretricious ring of worldly distinction.

Close to tears, I bent over to see whether anything could be done about my feet, and now perceived that they had slipped out of loose house shoes; at least a very big soft dark-red bedroom slipper lay behind me on the floor. I took it in my hand uncertainly, holding it by the heel, still strongly inclined to weep. It slipped away from me, I caught it as it fell—meanwhile, it had grown even larger —and now I held it by the toe.

All at once I had a feeling of inner release and realized the great value of the slipper, which was vibrating a little in my hand, weighted down by its heavy heel. How splendid to have such a limp red shoe, so soft and heavy! Experimentally I swung it a few times through the air, this was delicious and flooded me with ecstasy to the roots of my hair. A club, a blackjack, was nothing in comparison with my great shoe. Calziglione was the Italian name I called it.

When I gave the reddish-brown one a first playful blow on the head with Calziglione, the young irreproachable fell reeling to the divan, and the others and the room and the dreadful sea lost all their power over me. I was big and strong, I was free, and at the second blow to the reddish-brown one's head there was no longer any contest, there was no more need for demeaning self-defense in my actions but simple exultation and free lordly whim. Nor did

I now hate my vanquished foe in the least, I found him interesting, he was precious and dear to me, after all I was his master and his creator. For every good blow of my strange shoe-cudgel shaped that primitive and apelike head, forged it, rebuilt it, formed it; with every constructive impact it grew more attractive, handsomer, finer, became my creature and my work, a thing that satisfied me and that I loved. With a final expert blacksmith's blow I flattened the pointed occiput just enough. He was finished. He thanked me and stroked my hand. "It's all right," I said, waving to him. He crossed his hands over his breast and said obsequiously: "My name is Paul."

My breast swelled with a marvelous feeling of power, a feeling that expanded the space about me; the room—no more talk of "salon"!—shriveled with shame and crept emptily away. I stood beside the sea. The sea was blue-black, steel clouds pressed down upon the somber mountains, in the fiords the dark water boiled up foaming, storm squalls strayed in circles, compulsive and terrifying. I glanced up and raised my hand to signal that the storm could begin. A bolt of lightning bright and cold exploded out of the harsh blue, a warm typhoon descended howling, tumultuous gray forms streamed apart in the heavens like veined marble. Humpbacked waves rose terrifyingly from the tormented sea, the storm tore spindrift from their tops and stinging wisps of foam and whipped them in my face. The benumbed black mountains tore open eyes full of horror. Their silent cowering together rang out like a supplication.

In the midst of the magnificent charge of the storm,

mounted on gigantic, ghostly horses, a timid voice spoke close to me. Oh, I had not forgotten you, pale lady of the long black hair. I bent over to her and she spoke to me childishly—the sea was coming, one could not stay there. I was touched and continued to look at the gentle sinner, her face was only a quiet pallor amid the encircling twilight of her hair, then the chiding waves were already striking at my knees and at my breast, and the sinner floated helpless and silent on the rising waters. I laughed a little, put my arm under her knees, and raised her up to me. This too was beautiful and liberating, the woman was strangely light and small, full of fresh warmth and her eyes were sincere, trusting, and alarmed, and I saw that she was no sinner at all nor any distant, incomprehensible lady. No sins, no mystery; she was just a child.

Out of the waves and across the rocks I carried her and through the rain-darkened, royally grieving park, where the storm could not reach and where from the bowed crowns of ancient trees simple, softly human beauty spoke, pure poems and symphonies, a world of noble intimations and charmingly civilized delights, enchanting trees painted by Corot and noble rustic woodwind music by Schubert, which subtly tempted me to the beloved temple in a momentary upsurge of nostalgia. But in vain; the world has many voices, and the soul has its hours and its moments for everything.

God knows how the sinner, the pale woman, the child. took her leave and disappeared from sight. There was an outside stairway of stone, there was an entrance gate, there were servants present, all dim and cloudy as though behind translucent glass, and something else even more insubstantial, even more cloudy, figures blown there by the wind; a note of censure and reproach directed against me aroused my ire at that storm of shadows. All disappeared except the form of Paul, my friend and son Paul, and in his features was revealed and hidden a face unnamable and yet infinitely familiar, the face of a schoolmate, the primeval legendary face of a nursemaid, composed of the good nourishing half-memories of the fabulous earliest years.

Good heart-comforting darkness, warm cradle of the soul and lost homeland, opens before me, time of inchoate being, the first uncertain quiverings above the fountain's source, beneath which sleep ancient times with their dreams of tropical forests. Do but feel your way, soul, do but wander, plunge blindly into the rich bath of guiltless twilight desires! I know you, timid soul, nothing is more necessary to you, nothing is so much food, drink, and sleep for you, as the return to your beginnings. There the waves roar around you and you are a wave, the forest rustles and you are the forest, there is no outer, no inner any more, you fly, a bird in the air, you swim, a fish in the sea, you breathe in light and are light, taste darkness and are darkness. We wander, soul, we swim and fly and smile and, with delicate ghostly fingers, we retie the torn filaments and blissfully unite the disjointed harmonies. We no longer seek God. We are God. We are the world. We kill and die along with others, we create and are resurrected with our dreams. Our finest dream, that is the blue sky, our finest dream, that is the sea, our finest dream, that is the starlit night, and is the fish and is the bright happy light and bright happy sounds—everything is our dream, each is our finest dream. We have just died and become earth. We have just discovered laughter. We have just arranged a constellation.

Voices resound and each is the voice of our mother. Trees rustle, and each one of them rustled above our cradle. Roads diverge in a star pattern and each road leads toward home.

The one who had called himself Paul, my creature and my friend, was there again and had become as old as I was. He resembled a friend of my youth, but I did not know which one and therefore I was a little uneasy with him and showed him a certain courtesy. From this he drew power. The world no longer obeyed me, it obeyed him and therefore everything that had preceded had disappeared and collapsed in craven improbability, put to shame by him who governed now.

We were in a square, the place was called Paris, and in front of me an iron girder towered into the air; it was a ladder and on both sides were small iron rungs to which one could hold with one's hands and on which one could climb with one's feet. Since Paul desired it, I climbed first and he beside me on an identical ladder. When we had climbed as high as a house or a very high tree, I began to feel frightened. I looked over at Paul, he felt no fear but he recognized my own and smiled.

For the space of a breath while he smiled and I stared at him, I was very close to recognizing his face and remembering his name, a fissure in the past opened and split down to my schooldays, back to the time when I was twelve years old, life's most glorious period when everything was full of fragrance, everything was congenial, everything was gilded with an edible smell of fresh bread and an intoxicating shimmer of adventure—Jesus was twelve years old when he shamed the scribes in the temple, at twelve we have all shamed our scribes and teachers, have been smarter than they, more gifted than they, braver than they. Memories and images pressed in upon me. Forgotten schoolbooks, detention during the noon hour, a bird killed with a slingshot, a coat pocket stickily filled with stolen plums, wild, boyish splashings in the swimming hole, torn Sunday trousers and torments of conscience, ardent prayers at night about earthly problems, marvelous heroic feelings of magnificence on reading verses by Schiller. — —

It was only a second's lightning flash, avidly hurrying picture sequences without focus. In the next instant Paul's face stared at me again, tormentingly half recognized. I was no longer sure of my age, possibly we were boys. Farther and farther below the narrow rungs of our ladders lay the mass of streets that was called Paris. But when we were higher than any tower, our iron girders came to an end and proved to be surmounted, each of them, by a horizontal board, a minuscule platform. It seemed impossible to get on top of these. But Paul did it negligently, and I had to do it too.

Once on top I laid myself flat on the board and looked down over the edge as though from a high little cloud. My glance fell like a stone into emptiness and found no goal.

Then my comrade pointed with his hand and I became fascinated by a marvelous sight that hovered in midair. There, above a broad avenue at the level of the highest roofs but immensely far below us, I saw a foreign-looking company; they seemed to be high-wire dancers and indeed one of the figures was running to and fro on a wire or rod. Then I discovered that there were a great many of them, almost all young girls, and they seemed to me to be gypsies or other nomadic folk. They walked, lay, sat, moved at the height of the roofs on an airy framework of the thinnest scaffolding and arborlike poles, they lived there and were at home in that region. Beneath them the street could only be imagined, a fine swirling mist extended from the ground up almost to their feet.

Paul made some remark about it. "Yes," I replied, "it is pathetic, all those girls."

To be sure, I was much higher than they were, but I was clinging to my position and they moved lightly and fearlessly, and I saw that I was too high, I was in the wrong place. They were at the right height, not on the ground and yet not so devilishly high and distant as I was, not among people and yet not so completely isolated; moreover, there were many of them. I saw very well that they represented a bliss that I had not yet attained.

But I knew that sooner or later I would have to climb down my monstrous ladder and the thought of it was so oppressive that I felt nauseated and could not endure being up there for another instant. Desperate and shaking with dizziness, I felt beneath me with my feet for the rungs of the ladder—I could not see them from the board

—and for hideous minutes hung at that terrifying height struggling convulsively. No one helped me, Paul was gone.

In abject fear I executed hazardous kicks and graspings, and a feeling came over me like a fog, a feeling that it was not the high ladder or the dizziness that I had to endure and taste to the full. For almost at once I lost the sight and form of things, everything turned to fog and confusion. At one moment I was still hanging dizzily from the rungs, at the next I was creeping, small and frightened, through narrow underground passages and corridors, then I was wading hopelessly through mud and dung, feeling the filthy slime rising toward my mouth. Darkness and obstacles were everywhere. Dreadful tasks of grave but shrouded purport. Fear and sweat, paralysis and cold. Hard death, hard birth.

What endless night surrounds us! How many paths of torment we pursue, go deep into the cavern of our rubble-filled soul, eternal suffering hero, eternal Odysseus! But we go on, we go on, we bow ourselves and wade, we swim, choking in the slime, we creep along smooth noxious walls. We weep and despair, we whimper in fear and howl aloud in pain. But we go on, we go on and suffer, we go on and gnaw our way through.

Out of the seething hellish vapors visibility returned once more, a short stretch of the dark path was again revealed in the formative light of memory, and the soul forced its way out of the primeval world into the familiar circle of known time.

Where was this? Familiar objects gazed at me, I

breathed an atmosphere I recognized. A big room in half darkness, a kerosene lamp on the table, my own lamp, a big round table rather like a piano. My sister was there, and my brother-in-law, perhaps on a visit to me or perhaps I was with them. They were quiet and worried, full of concern about me. And I stood in the big dim room, walked back and forth, stopped and walked again in a cloud of sadness, in a flood of bitter, choking sadness. And now I began to look for something, nothing important, a book or a pair of scissors or something of that sort, and I could not find it. I took the lamp in my hand, it was heavy, and I was terribly weary, I soon put it down but then picked it up again and wanted to go on searching, searching, although I knew it was useless, I would find nothing, I would only increase confusion everywhere, the lamp would fall from my hands, it was so heavy, so painfully heavy, and so I would go on groping and searching and wandering through the room all my miserable life long.

My brother-in-law looked at me, worried and a little reproachful. They can see that I am going mad, I thought immediately, and picked up the lamp again. My sister came to me, silent with pleading eyes, full of fear and love, so that I felt my heart would break, I could say nothing, I could only stretch out my hand and wave her off, motion to her to stay away, and I thought: Just leave me alone! Just leave me alone! You cannot know how I feel, how I suffer, how frightfully I suffer! And again: Leave me alone! Just leave me alone!

The reddish lamplight dimly flooded the big room, outside the trees groaned in the wind. For an instant I seemed to have a most profound inward vision and sensation of the night outside: wind and wetness, autumn, the bitter smell of foliage, fluttering leaves from the elm tree, autumn, autumn! And once more for an instant I was not I myself but saw myself as though in a picture: I was a pale haggard musician with flickering eyes named Hugo Wolf and on this evening I was in the process of going mad.

Meanwhile, I had to go on searching, hopelessly searching, and lifting the heavy lamp onto the table, onto the chair, onto the bookcase. And I had to defend myself with beseeching gestures when my sister once more looked at me sadly and considerately, wanting to comfort me, wanting to be near me and help me. The sorrow within me grew and filled me to the bursting point, and the images around me were of eloquent, engrossing quality, much clearer than any ordinary reality; a few autumn flowers in a glass, with a dark reddish-brown mat beneath it, glowed with painfully beautiful loneliness, each thing, even the shining brass base of the lamp, was of an enchanted beauty and isolated by fateful separateness, as in the paintings of the great masters.

I saw my fate clearly. One deeper shade in this sadness, one further glance from my sister, one more look from the flowers, the beautiful soulful flowers—and the flood would come, I would sink into madness. "Leave me! You do not understand!" On the polished side of the piano a beam of lamplight was reflected in the dark wood, so beautiful, so mysterious, so filled with melancholy!

Now my sister rose again and went to the piano. I wanted to plead with her, I wanted to stop her by mental power but I could not, no sort of strength went out to her now from my loneliness. Oh, I knew what was certain to happen then, I knew the melody that would now inevitably find voice, saying all and destroying all. Monstrous tension compressed my heart, and while the first burning tears sprang from my eyes, I threw my head and hands across the table and listened to and absorbed with all my senses, and with newly added senses as well, the words and melody at once, Wolf's melody and the verses:

> *What do you know, dark treetops,*
> *Of the beauty of olden times?*
> *The homeland beyond the mountains,*
> *How far from us now, how far!*

At this, before my eyes and within me the world slid apart, was swallowed up in tears and tones, impossible to express the fluidity, the torrent, the beneficence and pain! O tears, O sweet collapse, blissful melting away! All the books of the world full of thoughts and poems are nothing in comparison with one minute's sobbing when feeling surges in waves, soul perceives and finds itself in the depths. Tears are the melting ice of the soul, all angels are close to one who weeps.

Forgetful of all causes and reasons, I wept my way down from the heights of unbearable tension into the gentle twilight of ordinary feelings, without thoughts, without witnesses. In between, images fluttered: a coffin in which lay a man very dear and important to me, but I knew not who. Perhaps you yourself, I thought; then another scene appeared to me from the far pale distance.

Had I not years ago or in an earlier life witnessed a marvelous sight: a company of young girls living high in the air, cloudlike and weightless, beautiful and blissful, floating light as air and rich as string music?

Years flew between, forcing me gently but irresistibly away from the picture. Alas, perhaps my whole life had had only this meaning, to see those lovely hovering maidens, to approach them, to become like them! Now they disappeared in the distance, unreachable, uncomprehended, unreleased, wearily encircled by fluttering desire and despair.

Years drifted down like snowflakes and the world was changed. I was wandering sadly toward a small house. I felt wretched, and an alarming sensation in my mouth preoccupied me, cautiously I poked my tongue at a doubtful tooth, which at once slipped sideways and fell out. The next one—it, too! A very young doctor was there, to whom I appealed, holding out one tooth in my fingers beseechingly. He laughed merrily, dismissing me with a deadly professional glance and shaking his young head—that doesn't amount to a thing, quite harmless, happens every day. Dear God, I thought. But he went on and pointed at my left knee: that's where the trouble was, that was something quite different and no joking matter. With panic speed I reached down to my knee—there it was! There was a hole into which I could thrust my finger, and instead of skin and flesh there was nothing to feel but an insensitive, soft, spongy mass, light and fibrous as the substance of wilted plants. O my God, this was destruction, this was death and disintegration! "So there's nothing more to be done?" I asked with painstaking friendliness. "Nothing more," said the young doctor and disappeared.

Exhausted, I walked toward the little house, not as desperate as I really should have been, in fact almost indifferent. Now I had to enter the little house where my mother was waiting for me—had I not already heard her voice? Seen her face? Steps led upward, crazy steps, high and smooth, without a railing, each one a mountain, each a summit, a glacier. It was certainly too late—perhaps she had already left, perhaps she was already dead? Had I not just heard her call again? Silently I struggled with the steep mountainous steps; falling and bruised, wild and sobbing, I climbed and strained, supporting myself on failing arms and knees, and was on top, was at the gate, and the steps were again small and pretty and bordered by boxwood. My every stride was sluggish and heavy as though through slime and glue, no getting on, the gate stood open, and within, wearing a gray dress, my mother walked, a little basket on her arm, silently sunk in thought. Oh, her dark, slightly graying hair in the little net! And her walk, the small figure! And the dress, the gray dress—had I completely lost her image for all those many many years, had I never properly thought of her at all? There she was, there she stood and walked, only visible from behind, exactly as she had been, very clear and beautiful, pure love, pure thoughts of love!

Furiously I waded through the sticky air with paralyzed gait, tendrils of plants curled round me like thin strong ropes tighter and tighter, malignant obstacles everywhere, no getting on! "Mother!" I cried. —But I had no voice

. . . No sound came. There was glass between her and me.

My mother walked on slowly without looking back, silently involved in beautiful loving thoughts, brushing with her familiar hand an invisible thread from her dress, bending over her little basket with her sewing materials. Oh, that little basket! In it she had once hidden an Easter egg for me. I cried out desperate and voiceless. I ran and could not leave the spot! Tenderness and rage consumed me.

And she walked on slowly through the summerhouse, stood in the open doorway on the other side, stepped out into the open. She let her head sink a little to one side, gently listening, absorbed in thoughts, raised and lowered the little basket—I recalled a slip of paper I had found as a boy in her sewing basket, on which she had written in her flowing hand what she planned to do that day and to take care of. "Hermann's trousers raveled out—put away laundry—borrow book by Dickens—yesterday Hermann did not say his prayers." Rivers of memory, cargoes of love!

Bound and chained, I stood at the gate, and beyond it the woman in the gray dress walked slowly away, into the garden, and disappeared.

Faldum

1. THE FAIR

THE ROAD leading to the city of Faldum wound through upland country, sometimes past forests or broad green meadows, sometimes past cornfields, and the nearer it came to the city, the more farms, dairies, gardens, and country houses it skirted. The sea was too far away to be seen, and the world seemed to consist of nothing but gentle hills, pretty little valleys, meadows and woods, farmlands and vegetable gardens. It was a country amply supplied with fruit and firewood, milk and meat, apples and nuts. The villages were charming and clean, the people on the whole were honest, diligent, and by no means inclined to dangerous or revolutionary enterprises, and everyone felt content if his neighbor prospered no better than himself. This was the nature of Faldum, and most places in the world are much the same so long as certain things do not happen to them.

The pretty road to the city of Faldum (the city had the same name as the country) on this particular morning had seen since first cockcrow livelier traffic both afoot and on horseback than at any other time of the year, for this was the day of the great annual fair in the city and for twenty miles around there was not a farmer or farmer's wife, not a master or apprentice or schoolboy, not a man-servant or maidservant, not a youth or maiden, who had not been thinking for weeks of the great fair and dreaming of going there. Not all could go, of course; someone had to look after the cattle and little children, the sick and the old, and whoever had been chosen to stay and take care of the house and property felt as if he were losing almost a year of his life and bitterly resented the beautiful sun that since early morning had shone warm and radiant in the blue sky of late summer.

Married women and girls hurried along with little baskets on their arms, the young men with clean-shaven cheeks had carnations or asters in their buttonholes, all were in Sunday attire, and the schoolgirls' carefully braided hair still shone wet and lustrous in the sunshine. Those driving carriages had a flower or a red ribbon tied around the handles of their whips, and whoever could afford it had decorated the harness of his horses with strings of brightly polished brass disks that reached to the horses' knees. Rack wagons came by with green roofs of beech boughs arching over them, and crowded underneath, people sat with baskets or children in their laps, most of them singing loudly in chorus. There appeared now and again a wagon especially gay, with its banners and paper flowers, red, blue, and white among the green beech leaves, and from it village music swelled and echoed and between its boughs in the half shadow glinted and sparkled golden horns and trumpets. Little children who had been dragged along since sunrise began to cry and were comforted by their perspiring mothers, and many were given lifts by good-natured drivers. An old woman was pushing twins in a baby carriage, both asleep, and on the pillow between the sleeping children lay two beautifully dressed and combed dolls with cheeks no less round and rosy.

Anyone living along the road who was not going to the fair that day had an entertaining morning with this continuous procession of sights. However, these stay-at-homes were few in number. A ten-year-old youngster sitting on the garden stairs was weeping because he had to remain with his grandmother, but when he saw a couple of village boys trotting past he decided that he had sat and wept long enough and sprang down onto the road to join them. Not far from there lived an elderly bachelor who didn't want to hear a thing about the fair because he begrudged the money. He had planned, while everybody was away celebrating that day, to trim the high whitethorn hedge around his garden in peace and quiet, for the hedge needed it, and hardly had the morning dew begun to evaporate when he had gone cheerily to work with his long hedge shears. But he had stopped after barely an hour and angrily sought refuge in his house, for no man or boy had gone past, walking or riding, without looking in astonishment at the hedge-cutter and making some joke about his ill-timed diligence, at which the girls had giggled; and when he had threatened them furiously with his long shears, they had all waved their hats and laughed at him. Now he was sitting inside behind closed shutters, peering out enviously through the cracks, but his anger subsided in time, and as the last few fairgoers bustled and hurried by as though their lives depended on it, he pulled on his boots, put a taler in his pouch, picked up his walking stick, and was about to set out. Then it suddenly occurred to him that a taler was after all a lot of money; he removed it and instead put a half taler into his leather pouch and tied it up. He thrust the pouch into his pocket, locked the house and the garden gate, and ran so fast that he reached the city ahead of many of the pedestrians and even overtook two wagons.

With him gone and the house and garden deserted, the dust over the road gently began to settle; the sound of hoofs and the band music had faded away in the distance and already the sparrows were coming out of the fields of stubble, bathing in the white dust and surveying what was left over from the tumult. The road lay empty and dead and hot; from the far distance from time to time, faint and lost, came a shout or the notes of a horn.

Then a man strolled out of the forest, his broad-brimmed hat pulled low over his eyes, and he wandered unhurriedly and alone along the empty country road. He was tall and had the firm quiet stride of a hiker who has traveled great distances afoot. He was dressed inconspicuously in gray and out of the shadow of his hat his eyes peered attentive and calm, the eyes of one who desires nothing more from the world but observes everything scrupulously and overlooks nothing. He took note of the innumerable confused wagon tracks running along the road, the hoof marks of a horse that had thrown the shoe from its left hind foot; in the distance through the dusty haze he saw the roofs of the city of Faldum, small and shimmering, on the top of a hill; he saw a little old woman, full of anxiety and fear, rushing around a garden calling to someone who did not answer. On the edge of the road the sun flashed from a piece of metal and he bent to pick up a bright round brass disk that had come from a horse collar. He put this in his pocket. And then he saw standing beside the road an old whitethorn hedge which for a few paces had been freshly trimmed; at the start the work seemed neat and precise as if executed with pleasure, but with each half stride it grew less even and soon a cut had gone too deep, neglected twigs were sticking up bristly and thorny. Farther on, the stranger found a child's doll lying in the road with its head crushed by a wagon wheel, then a piece of rye bread still gleaming with melted butter; and finally he found a heavy leather pouch in which there was a half taler. He leaned the doll against a curbstone, crumbled up the slice of bread and fed it to the sparrows, but the pouch with the half taler he thrust into his pocket.

It was indescribably quiet on the abandoned road, the turf on either side lay gray with dust in the sun. Nearby in a farmyard the chickens ran around, with no one to mind, cackling and stuttering dreamily in the warm sun. An old woman was stooping over a bluish cabbage patch, pulling weeds out of the dry soil. The wanderer called to her to ask how far it was to the city. But she was deaf, and when he called louder she only looked at him helplessly and shook her gray head.

As he walked on, from time to time music reached him from the city, swelling and then dying away, then it came oftener and for longer periods, and finally it sounded un-interruptedly, like a distant waterfall, music and a confusion of voices, as though a parliament of mankind were happily assembled up there. A stream now ran beside the road, broad and quiet, with ducks swimming on it and brownish-green waterweed under the blue surface. Then the road began to climb, the stream curved to one side and a stone bridge led across it. A thin man who looked like a tailor was sitting asleep with drooping head on the low wall of the bridge; his hat had fallen off into the dust and beside him sat a droll little dog keeping watch. The stranger was about to waken the sleeper lest he fall off the wall of the bridge in his sleep. But on looking down he saw that the height was moderate and the water shallow; and so he let the tailor go on sleeping undisturbed.

Now after a short steep rise in the road the stranger came to Faldum's city gate, which stood wide open, with no one in sight. He strode through, his steps resounding suddenly and loudly on the paved street where in front of the houses on both sides stood rows of empty, unharnessed wagons and caleches. From other streets came noise and confused shouting, but here there was no one, the little street lay in shadow and only the upper windows of the houses reflected the golden day. The wanderer sat down on the pole of a rack wagon for a short rest. When he got up to leave, he placed on the driver's seat the brass harness decoration he had found in the road.

He had gone barely a block farther along when he was engulfed in the noise and confusion of the fair. In a hundred booths dealers loudly hawked their wares, children blew on silvery trumpets, butchers fished long necklaces of fresh wet sausages out of huge boiling kettles, a quack stood on a high platform peering encouragingly through thick horn-rimmed glasses and pointing to a chart on which were inscribed all sorts of human diseases and ailments. A man with long black hair walked past, leading a camel by a rope. The animal looked down arrogantly from its long neck on the crowds of people and twisted its divided lips back and forth as it chewed.

The man who had come out of the woods looked attentively at all this, allowed himself to be pushed and shoved along by the people, glanced now into the stand of a dealer in colored prints, then read sayings and mottoes on sugared gingerbread, but he lingered nowhere and seemed not yet to have found what presumably he was looking for. And so he proceeded slowly and came to the big central square, where a bird dealer had set up shop on one corner. He listened for a while to the voices that came from the many little cages, and he answered them, whistling softly to the linnet, the quail, the canary, the warbler.

Suddenly he saw nearby a bright flash of light, as brilliant and blinding as though all the sunshine had been concentrated at this one point, and when he approached, it turned out to be a big mirror hanging in an exhibitor's booth, and beside it were other mirrors, tens and dozens and more, big, small, rectangular, round, oval, mirrors to be hung on the wall, mirrors on stands, hand mirrors and little narrow pocket mirrors that you could have with you so as not to forget your own face. The dealer was standing there manipulating a sparkling hand mirror so that the reflection of the sun danced around his booth; meanwhile, he shouted tirelessly: "Mirrors, ladies and gentlemen. This is the place to buy mirrors! The best mirrors, the cheapest mirrors in Faldum! Mirrors, ladies, magnificent mirrors! Just take a look at them, all genuine, all of the best crystal!"

The stranger stopped beside the mirror booth as if he had found what he was looking for. Among the people inspecting the mirrors were three young country girls; he took up a position close to them and saw that they were fresh, healthy peasants, neither beautiful nor ugly, in thick-soled shoes and white stockings, with blond, rather sun-faded plaits and eager young eyes. Each of the three was holding a mirror in her hand, not one of the large or expensive ones, and while they hesitated over the purchase and enjoyed the pleasurable torment of choice, each would gaze forlornly and dreamily into the clear depths of the mirror, surveying her image, her mouth and eyes, the little ornament at her throat, the sprinkling of freckles across the bridge of her nose, the smooth hair, the rosy ear. They became silent and solemn; the stranger who was standing just behind them saw their large-eyed, serious faces peering out of the three mirrors.

"Oh, how I wish," he heard the first one say, "how I wish I had hair that was all red-gold and long enough to reach to my knees!"

The second girl, hearing her friend's wish, sighed softly and looked more intently into her mirror. Then, blushing, she timidly divulged what her heart dreamed of: "If I had a wish, I would like to have the prettiest hands, all white and delicate, with long narrow fingers and rosy fingernails." She glanced down at the hand that was holding the oval mirror; though not ugly, it was rather short and broad and had become roughened and coarse from work.

The third, the smallest and merriest of the three, laughed and cried gaily: "That's not a bad wish. But you know hands aren't so important. What I'd like most is to be, from today on, the best and nimblest dancer in the whole country of Faldum."

Then the girl gave a sudden start and turned around, for out of the mirror, behind her own face, peered a stranger's face with gleaming black eyes, the face of the man from the forest, whom the three had not seen standing behind them until now. They stared at him with amazement as he nodded and said: "You have made three nice wishes, young ladies. Are you really serious about them?"

The small girl had put down the mirror and hidden her hands behind her back. She wanted to pay the man back for startling her, and was trying to think of a sharp rejoinder; but when she looked into his face, there was such power in his eyes that she grew confused. "Is it any business of yours what I wish?" was all she could say, blushing.

But the one who had wished for beautiful hands was impressed by the tall man's dignified and fatherly air. She said: "Yes, indeed, I am serious about it. Could one wish for anything finer?"

The mirror dealer had approached, other people too were listening. The stranger pushed back the brim of his hat so that his smooth high forehead and imperious eyes were strikingly visible. Now he nodded and smiled at the three girls and cried: "Just look, now you have everything you wished for!"

The girls stared at one another, then each looked quickly into a mirror, and they all grew pale with astonishment and joy. The first one had thick gold locks reaching to her knees. The second held her mirror in the whitest, slimmest princess hands, and the third was suddenly standing in red leather dancing shoes on ankles as slim as those of a doe. They could not grasp what had happened, but the one with the beautiful hands burst into blissful tears, leaned on the shoulder next to her, and wept happily into her friend's long hair. Now people began shouting, and news of the miracle was cried abroad from the neighborhood of the booth. A young journeyman who had seen the whole thing stood there staring at the stranger with wide-open eyes as though he had been turned to stone.

"Wouldn't you like to wish something for yourself?" the stranger suddenly asked him.

The apprentice gave a start, became totally confused, and let his eyes rove about helplessly, trying to spy something he could wish for. Then he saw hanging in front of the pork butcher's booth a great wreath of thick red knackwurst and he stammered, pointing at it: "A string of knackwurst like that, that's what I'd like to have!" And behold, there the wreath hung around his neck, and all who saw it began to laugh and shout, and everyone tried to press closer, everyone wanting to make a wish, and they were all allowed to. The next to have a turn was bolder and wished for a new outfit from top to toe; hardly had he spoken when he was dressed in brand-new clothing as fine as the burgermeister's. Then came a country woman who took her courage in both hands and asked straight out for ten talers, and forthwith the talers were jingling in her purse.

Now people saw that in all truth miracles were happening and at once the news spread from the marketplace across the city, and a huge group quickly formed around the booth of the mirror dealer. Many were still laughing and joking, wouldn't believe a word of it, and made skeptical remarks. But many had succumbed to the wish fever and came rushing with glowing eyes and faces hot and contorted with greed and worry, for each feared that the source might dry up before he had a chance to participate. Boys wished for cookies, crossbows, dogs, bags full of nuts, books, and games of bowls; girls went away happy with new clothes, ribbons, gloves, and parasols. A little ten-year-old boy who had run away from his grandmother and was quite beside himself with the sheer splendor and glamour of the fair wished in a clear voice for a live horse, a black one; and forthwith behind him was a black colt whinnying and rubbing his head affectionately on the boy's shoulder.

An elderly bachelor with a walking stick in his hand,

quivering with excitement and hardly able to speak a word, forced his way through the miracle-intoxicated throng.

"I wi-wish," he stammered, "I wi-wish for myself twice one hundred—"

The stranger looked at him closely, took a leather pouch from his pocket, and held it in front of the excited man's eyes. "Wait a minute!" he said. "Didn't you perhaps lose this money pouch? There's a half taler in it."

"Yes, I certainly did," cried the bachelor. "That's mine."

"Do you want it back again?"

"Yes, yes, give it here!"

So he got his pouch back again and thus used up his wish, and when he understood this he went at the stranger furiously with his cane, but did not succeed in hitting him; instead, he knocked down one of the mirrors and the fragments had not yet ceased rattling when the dealer was standing there demanding money, and the bachelor had to pay.

Then a corpulent householder stepped forward and made a capital wish—to wit, a new roof for his house. Immediately brand-new tiles and whitewashed chimneys were visible, shining in his street. Then everyone became feverish again and their wishes were pitched higher, and soon there was a man who felt no shame in making the modest wish for a new four-story house on the market-place, and in a quarter of an hour he was leaning over his own windowsill and watching the fair from that vantage point.

It was now really no longer a fair; instead, all the life of the city, like a river from a spring, flowed only from that spot beside the mirror booth where one could get a wish from the stranger. Cries of wonder, envy, or derision greeted each wish, and when a hungry little boy had wished for nothing but a hatful of plums, his hat was filled again with taler pieces by someone who had made a less modest wish. Great rejoicing and applause broke out when the fat wife of a storekeeper made use of her wish to cure herself of a large goiter. But then came an example of what anger and jealousy can do. The woman's husband, the shopkeeper, who lived in conflict with her and had just had a fight with her, made use of his own wish, which might have made him rich, to restore the vanished goiter to its old place. But the precedent had been set, and crowds of the sick and infirm were fetched and people fell into new frenzies as the lame began to dance and the blind ecstatically greeted the light with reawakened eyes.

Meanwhile, youngsters had run about everywhere announcing the miraculous happenings. The story was told of a loyal old cook who was standing at the hearth roasting a goose for her employers when she heard the news through the open window. She could not resist running off to the marketplace in order to wish herself rich and happy for life. But the farther along she pressed in the crowd the more tormented her conscience became, and when it was her turn to wish she gave up her plan and only requested that the goose might not burn up before she got back home.

The tumult would not cease. Nursemaids came rushing out of houses with their little ones in their arms, invalids stormed eagerly into the streets in their nightgowns. In a state of great confusion and despair, a little old lady made her way in from the country and when she heard about the wishing she begged in tears that she might find her lost grandchild safe and sound. Behold, without an instant's delay there came the boy riding on a little black horse and fell laughing into her arms.

Finally the whole city was transformed and overcome by intoxication. Pairs of lovers, their wishes fulfilled, wandered happily arm in arm; families rode in caleches, still wearing the old mended clothes they had put on that morning. Many who were already regretting unwise wishes had either sadly disappeared or drunk themselves into forgetfulness at the old fountain in the marketplace, which a prankster through his wish had supplied with the best wine.

And in the whole city of Faldum there were only two people who knew nothing about the miracle and had not made wishes for themselves. These were two young men who were behind closed windows high up in an attic room of an old house on the edge of town. One of them stood in the middle of the room with a violin under his chin and played with utter surrender of body and soul; the other sat in a corner with his head in his hands, totally absorbed in listening. Through the little windowpanes the beams of the late afternoon sun obliquely lit a bunch of flowers standing on the table and played over the torn wallpaper. The room was completely suffused with warm light and the glowing tones of the violin, like a little secret treasure chamber filled with the glitter of gems. The violinist's eyes were closed and he swayed back and forth as he played. The listener stared at the floor, lost in the music, as motionless as though there were no life in him.

Then footsteps sounded in the street and the house gate was thrown open and someone pounded heavily up the stairs all the way to the attic room. It was the owner of the house, who tore the door open and came shouting and laughing into the room. The music abruptly ceased; the silent listener leaped up startled and distressed, the violinist too was angry at being disturbed. But the landlord paid no heed, he swung his arms about like a drunkard and shouted: "Fools, there you sit fiddling and outside the whole world is being changed. Wake up and run so you won't be too late—there's a man in the marketplace who makes a wish come true for everyone. So you needn't live under the roof any more and continue to owe me the miserable bit of rent. Up and away before it's too late! I too have become a rich man today."

The violinist heard this with astonishment, but since the man would not leave him in peace, he set his violin aside and put his hat on his head; his friend followed silently. Barely were they out of the house when they saw the most remarkable changes in the city. They walked bemused, as though in a dream, past houses that only yesterday had been gray and askew and mean but now stood tall and elegant as palaces. People they had known as beggars drove by in four-horse carriages or looked in proud affluence out of the windows of beautiful homes. An emaciated fellow, who looked like a tailor and was followed by a tiny dog, was sweating as he wearily dragged behind him a great heavy sack, from which gold pieces trickled through a small hole onto the pavement. As though drawn by some magnet, the two youths arrived in the market-place and in front of the booth with the mirrors. There stood the strange man and he said to them: "You're in no hurry with your wishes. I was just about to leave. Well, tell me what you want and don't feel any hesitation."

The violinist shook his head and said: "Oh, if they'd only left me alone! I don't need anything."

"You don't? Think again!" cried the stranger. "You may wish for anything at all, anything you can think of."

The violinist closed his eyes for a moment and re-flected. Then he said softly: "I would like a violin on which I could play so marvelously that the whole world with its uproar could no longer come near me."

And behold, he was already holding a priceless violin and a bow in his hands, and he tucked the violin under his chin and began to play: it sang sweet and strong like the song of Paradise. Whoever heard it stopped and listened and his eyes grew solemn. But the violinist, playing more and more intensely and beautifully, was swept away by Those Who Are Invisible and disappeared in the air, and still from a great distance his music came drifting back with a soft radiance like the glow of sunset.

"And you? What do you wish for yourself?" the stranger asked the other young man.

"Now you have taken the violinist away from me!" the youth said. "I want nothing from life but to listen and watch, and I would like to think only about what is immortal. And so I would like to be a mountain as big as the countryside of Faldum and so tall that my summit would tower above the clouds."

Then a thundering began beneath the earth and everything started to shudder. There was a sound of breaking glass, the mirrors fell one after another into splinters on the pavement, and the marketplace rose swaying like a cloth under which a cat has suddenly awakened and is arching her back. An immense terror seized the people, thousands fled screaming out of the city into the fields. But those who remained in the market square saw behind the city a mighty mountain rising up into the evening clouds, and they saw the quiet stream transformed into a wild white torrent that rushed down foaming from high up on the mountain, with many falls and rapids, into the valley below.

Only a moment had passed, and the whole countryside of Faldum had become a gigantic mountain with the city lying at its foot, and now far away one could see the ocean. However, no one had been injured.

An old man standing beside the mirror booth, who had seen the whole thing, said to his neighbor: "The world's gone mad. I'm glad I haven't much longer to live. Only I'm sorry about the violinist. I would have liked to hear him play once more."

"Yes, indeed," said the other. "But tell me, what has become of the stranger?"

They looked all around. He had disappeared. But when they gazed up at the new mountain they saw the stranger walking away, his cape waving in the wind; they saw him stand for an instant, gigantic against the evening sky, and then vanish behind a cliff.

2. THE MOUNTAIN

Everything perishes, and all new things grow old. That annual fair was a thing of the past, and many a man who had wished himself rich on that occasion had long since grown poor again. The girl with the long red-gold hair had acquired a husband and children, who themselves had visited the fair in the city in the late summer of each year. The girl with the nimble dancing feet had married a master workman, she could still dance magnificently, better than many young people, and although her husband had wished himself a great deal of money, it looked as though this merry couple would run through it all within their lifetimes. But the third girl, the one with the beautiful hands, it was she who still thought more than anyone else about the stranger at the mirror booth. Indeed, this girl had never married and had not grown rich, but she still had her delicate hands and on their account no longer did farm work but tended the children of the village wherever she was needed and told them fairy tales and stories, and it was from her that all the children had learned about the miraculous fair and how the poor had become rich and the countryside of Faldum had become a mountain. When she told these stories she looked smilingly straight at her slender princess hands and was so lively and charming that one could believe there had been no luckier or more splendid prize given out at the mirror booth than hers, although she remained poor and husbandless and had to tell her beautiful stories to other people's children.

Everyone who had been young at that time was now old, and whoever had been old then had now died. Only the mountain was unaltered and ageless, and when the snow on its summit sparkled through the clouds, it seemed to smile and be happy that it was no longer a man and did not have to reckon in terms of human time. High above the city shone the mountain's cliffs, its huge shadow moved each day across the land, its brooks and rivers brought down advance notice of the waxing and waning of the seasons, the mountain had become the protector and father of all. Forests grew on it and meadows with waving grass and flowers; springs gushed forth from it and snow and ice and stones, and on the stones grew bright moss and beside the brooks forget-me-nots. Within the mountain were caverns where with unchanging music water dripped in silver threads year after year from stone to stone, and in its crevasses were secret chambers where with millennial patience crystals grew. On the summit of the mountain no man had ever stood. But many claimed to know that up there at the very top was a small round lake in which nothing had ever been mirrored except the sun, the moon, the clouds, and the stars. Neither man nor animal had ever looked into this pool which the mountain held up to the heavens, for even eagles could not fly so high.

The people of Faldum lived happily in their city and in

the many valleys; they christened their children, they carried on trade and commerce, they bore one another to the grave. And all that was handed on from forefathers to grandchildren and continued as a living tradition was their knowledge and their dreams about the mountain. Shepherds and chamois hunters, naturalists and botanists, mountain cowherds and travelers increased the treasure, and the makers of songs and tellers of tales spread it abroad; they learned of endless Stygian caves, of sunless waterfalls in hidden chasms, of towering glaciers, they learned the paths of the avalanches and the tricks of the weather, and everything the land received by way of warmth and frost, water and growth, weather and wind, all came from the mountain.

No one any longer knew about the earlier times. To be sure, there was the beautiful saga of the miraculous annual fair at which each soul in Faldum had been allowed to wish for whatever he wanted, but that the mountain had been formed on that day no one would now believe. The mountain, they knew for certain, had stood in its place from the beginning of time and would remain there for all eternity. The mountain was home, the mountain was Faldum. But the stories about the three girls and about the violin player, these the people loved to hear, and every once in a while there had been here or there a youth who would lock his door and lose himself in his violin playing as he dreamed of vanishing in his most beautiful song like the violin player who had been swept away into heaven.

The mountain lived on, silent and immense. Each day

it saw the sun rise distant and red out of the ocean and pursue its circular course past its summit from east to west, and each night it watched the stars following the same silent track. Each year winter wrapped it heavily with snow and ice, and each year in their season the avalanches thundered on their way and at the edges of their melting snows the bright-eyed summer flowers, blue and yellow, laughed in the sun and the brooks were in spate and the lakes shone blue and warm in the sunlight. In viewless caverns, lost waterfalls roared and the small round lake high above on the summit lay under heavy ice and waited all year for the brief period of high summer when for a few days it opened its bright blue eye to the sun and for a few nights reflected the stars. Dark caverns where stood the waters resounded with the unceasing fall of drops on stone, and in secret shafts the thousand-year-old crystals grew steadfastly toward perfection.

In the foothills of the mountain, a little higher than the city, lay a valley through which a broad stream with a smooth surface flowed between alders and willows. Thither went the young people who were in love and they learned from the mountain and the trees the marvel of the seasons. In another valley men trained with horses and weapons, and on a high steep promontory a mighty fire burned each year during the night of the summer solstice.

Ages slipped by and the mountain safeguarded the lovers' valley and the field of arms, he gave a home to cowherds and woodsmen, hunters and lumbermen; he provided stone for building and iron for smelting. Indifferent and permissive, he watched the first summer fire blaze on the promontory and saw it return a hundred times and many hundred times again. He saw the city down below reach out with little stumpy arms and grow beyond its ancient walls. He saw the hunters discard their crossbows and take up firearms. The centuries ran past him like the seasons of the year, and the years like hours.

It caused him no concern that in the long course of years a time came when the red solstice fire did not blaze on the smooth rock and from then on remained forgotten. He was not worried when in the march of the ages the field of arms was deserted and plantain and thistles overgrew the lists. And he did nothing to interfere when in the long course of the centuries a landslide altered his form and half the city of Faldum was reduced to rubble under the thundering rocks. He barely glanced down and did not even notice that the city lay there in ruins and no one rebuilt it.

All this disturbed him not at all. But something else did begin to worry him. The ages had slipped by and, behold, the mountain had grown old. When he saw the sun rise and move across the sky and depart, it was not the way it had once been, and when he saw the stars reflected in the pale glaciers he no longer felt himself their equal. Neither the sun nor the stars were any longer especially important to him; what was important now was what was happening to himself and within himself. For he could feel deep beneath his cliffs and caverns an alien hand at work, hard primitive rock grew friable and weathered into flaky slates as streams and waterfalls ate their way deeper. The glaciers had disappeared, the lakes had broadened, forests had been transformed into boulder fields and meadows into black moors; the barren ribbons of his moraines extended vastly far out into the country in pointed tongues, and the landscape below was strangely altered, had become oddly stony, blasted and silent. The mountain withdrew more and more into himself. He was clearly no longer the equal of the sun and the stars, his equals were wind and snow, water and ice. Whatever seems eternal and yet slowly wears away and perishes, that was his equal.

He began to guide his brooks more affectionately down into the valley, he rolled his avalanches with greater caution, he offered his flowery meadows more solicitously to the sun. And it happened that in his advanced age he also remembered men again. Not that he thought of men as equals, but he began to look about for them, he began to feel abandoned and to think about the past. But the city was no longer there, there were no songs in the valley of love, and no huts on the mountain peaks. There were no more men. All had gone. All had grown still, had become parched, a shadow lay in the air.

The mountain shuddered when he realized what dissolution meant; and as he shuddered, his summit bent to one side and pitched down and the rocky fragments rolled after it across the valley of love, long since filled up with stones, down into the sea.

Yes, times had changed. Why was it that just now he had to remember men and think about them continually? Had it not once been very beautiful when the fire on the promontory had burned and the young people in pairs had wandered through the valley of love? And oh, how sweet and warm their songs had sounded!

The ancient mountain was wholly sunk in memories, he hardly noticed the centuries flowing by, how here and there in his caverns there was subsidence accompanied by collisions and a soft thundering. When he thought about men he was pained by a dull echo from past ages of the world, a not-understood inclination and love, a dim intermittent dream as though once he too had been a man or like men, had sung and heard others sing, as though the idea of mortality had once in his earliest days transfixed his heart.

The ages flowed by. In collapse and surrounded by a barren wasteland of rubble, the dying mountain gave himself up to his dreams. How had that once been? Was there not still a resonance, a slender silver thread that united him with the bygone world? Laboriously he burrowed in the night of moldering memories, groping ceaselessly for torn threads, repeatedly bending far out over the abyss of things past. —Had there not been for him too, in the very distant ages past, the glow of friendship, of love? Had not he too, the lonely one, the great one, once been an equal among equals? —Had not once at the beginning of the world a mother sung to him too?

He brooded and brooded, and his eyes, the blue lakes, grew cloudy and dull and turned into moor and swamp, and over the strips of grass and little patches of flowers swept the rolling boulders. He continued to brood, and from an unimaginable distance he heard a chime ringing, felt the notes of music around him, a song, a human song, and he trembled with the painful joy of recognition. He heard the notes and he saw a man, a youth, wholly enveloped in music, poised in midair in the sunny sky, and a hundred buried memories were aroused and began to quiver and stir. He saw a human face with dark eyes, and the eyes asked commandingly: "Do you not want to make a wish?"

And he made a wish, a silent wish, and as he did so, he was freed from the torment of having to think about all those lost and distant things, and everything fell from him that had caused him pain. The mountain collapsed and with it the country, and where Faldum had been, the illimitable sea tossed and roared, and over it in steady alternation moved the sun and the stars.

Iris

IN THE SPRINGTIDE of his childhood Anselm used to run and play in the green garden. One of his mother's flowers called the sword lily was his special favorite. He used to press his cheek against the tall, bright-green leaves, touch their sharp points with exploratory fingers, deeply inhale the scent of the marvelous large blooms, and stare into them for minutes at a time. Within, there were long rows of yellow fingers rising from the pale blue floor of the flower, and between them ran a bright path far downward into the calyx and the remote blue mystery of the blossom. He had a great love for this flower and peering into it was his favorite pastime; sometimes he saw the delicate upright yellow members as a golden fence in a king's garden, sometimes as a double row of beautiful dream trees untouched by any breeze, and between them, bright and interlaced with living veins as delicate as glass, ran the mysterious path to the interior. There at the back the cavern yawned hugely and the path between the golden trees lost itself infinitely deep in unimaginable abysses, the violet vault arched royally above it and cast thin, magic shadows on the silent, expectant marvel. Anselm knew that this was the flower's mouth, that behind the luxuriant yellow finery in the blue abyss lived her heart and thoughts, and that along this lovely shining path with its glassy veins her breath and dreams flowed to and fro.

Alongside the tall flower stood smaller ones which had not yet opened; they rose on firm, sap-filled stems in little chalices of brownish-yellow skin, out of which the new blossoms forced their way upward silently and vigorously, wrapped tight in bright-green and lilac, but at the very top the new deep violet, erect and neatly rolled, peered out in delicate points, and even these young, tight-rolled petals showed a network of veins and a hundred secret signs.

In the morning when he came out of the house, fresh from sleep and dreams and strange worlds, there stood the garden waiting for him, never lost yet always new, and where yesterday there had been the hard blue point of a blossom tightly rolled, staring out of its green sheath, now hung thin and blue as air a young petal with a tongue and a lip, tentatively searching for the curving form of which it had long dreamed. At the very bottom where it was still engaged in a noiseless struggle with its sheath, delicate yellow growth was already in preparation, the bright veined path and the far-off fragrant abyss of the soul. Perhaps as early as midday, perhaps by evening, it would open, the blue silk tent would unfold over the golden forest, and her first dreams, thoughts, and songs would be breathed silently out of the magical abyss.

There came a day when the grass was full of blue bell-flowers. There came a day when suddenly there were new sounds and a new fragrance in the garden, and over the reddish, sun-drenched leaves hung the first tea rose, soft and golden red. There came a day when there were no more sword lilies. They were gone; there were no more gold-fenced paths leading gently down into fragrant mysteries, and the cool pointed leaves stood stark and unfriendly. But red berries were ripening in the bushes, and above the starflowers flew new, unheard-of butterflies, joyous and unconfined, reddish-brown ones with mother-of-pearl backs, and whirring, glassy-winged hawk moths.

Anselm talked to the butterflies and the pebbles, he made friends with the beetles and lizards, birds told him bird stories, ferns secretly revealed to him under the roof of their giant fronds their stores of brown seeds; for him fragments of green and crystal glass, catching the sun's rays, turned into palaces, gardens, and sparkling treasure chambers. With the lilies gone, the nasturtiums bloomed; when the tea roses wilted, then brambles grew brown. Everything changed places, was always there and always gone, disappeared and came again in its season, and even those marvelous frightening days, when the wind whistled chilly through the pine forest and in the whole garden the wilted foliage rattled very sear and dead, brought still another song, a new experience, a story, until once more all subsided, snow fell outside the windows and palm forests grew on the panes, angels with silver bells flew through the evening, and hall and attic were redolent of dried fruit. Friendship and confidence never failed in that good world, and when snowdrops unexpectedly shone beside the black ivy leaves, then it was as though they had been there all the time. Until one day, never expected and yet always exactly the way it had to be and always equally welcome, the first pointed bluish bud peeped out again from the stem of the sword lily.

To Anselm everything was beautiful, everything was delightful, friendly, and familiar, but his highest moment of magic and of grace came each year with the first sword lily. At some moment in his earliest childhood he had read in her chalice for the first time the book of marvels, her fragrance and changing, multifarious blue had been summons and key to the universe. Thus the sword lily had gone with him through all the years of his innocence, had become new with each new summer, richer in mystery and more moving. Other flowers too had mouths, others diffused fragrance and thoughts, others too enticed bees and beetles into their small sweet chambers. But to the boy the blue lily had become dearer and more important than any other flower, she was for him the symbol and example of everything worth contemplating and marveling at. When he stared into her chalice and in absorption allowed his thoughts to follow that bright dreamlike path between the marvelous yellow shrubbery toward the twilight interior of the flower, then his soul looked through the gate where appearance becomes a paradox and seeing a surmise. Sometimes at night too he dreamed of this flowery chalice, saw it opening gigantically in front of him, like the gate of a heavenly palace, and through it he would ride on horseback, would fly on swans, and with him flew and rode and glided gently the whole world drawn by magic into the lovely abyss, inward and downward, where every expectation had to find fulfillment and every intimation came true.

Each phenomenon on earth is an allegory, and each allegory is an open gate through which the soul, if it is ready, can pass into the interior of the world where you and I and day and night are all one. In the course of his life, every human being comes upon that open gate, here or there along the way; everyone is sometime assailed by the thought that everything visible is an allegory and that behind the allegory live spirit and eternal life. Few, to be sure, pass through the gate and give up the beautiful illusion for the surmised reality of what lies within.

Thus to the boy Anselm the chalice of his flower seemed to be the open, unvoiced question toward which his soul was striving in growing anticipation of a blessed answer. Then the lovely multiplicity of things drew him away again, in conversation and games with glass and stones, roots, bushes, animals, and all the friendly presences of his world. Often he was sunk in deep contemplation of himself, he would sit with closed eyes absorbed in the marvels of his own body, feeling as he swallowed, as he sang, as he breathed, strange sensations, impulses, and intimations in mouth and throat, groping too for the path and the gate by which soul can go to soul. With amazement he observed the colored figures full of meaning which appeared to him out of the purple darkness when he closed his eyes, spots and half circles of blue and deep red with glassy-bright lines between. Sometimes Anselm realized with a happy start the subtle hundredfold interconnections between eye and ear, smell and taste; he felt for beautiful fleeting instants tones, noises, and letters of the alphabet related and very similar to red and blue, to hard and soft; or he marveled, as he smelled some plant or peelings of green bark, at how strangely close smell and taste lie together and often cross over into one another and become one.

All children feel this, although not all with the same intensity and delicacy, and with many the feeling is gone and as though it had never existed even before they have learned to read their first letters. Others retain the mystery of childhood for a long time and a vestige and echo of it stays with them into the days of white hair and weariness. All children, as long as they remain within this mystery, are uninterruptedly occupied in their souls with the single important thing, with themselves and their paradoxical relationship to the outside world. Seekers and wise men return to this preoccupation in their mature years; most people, however, forget and abandon, early and for good, this inner world of the truly important, and all their lives long wander about in the many-colored mazes of wishes, worries, and goals, none of which has a place in their innermost being and none of which leads them back to their innermost being or to home.

During Anselm's childhood, summers and autumns softly came and went, again and again the snowdrops, wallflowers, violets, lilies, periwinkles, and roses bloomed and faded, beautiful and luxuriant as always. He lived together with them; flower and bird, tree and spring listened to him, and he took his first written letters and the first woes of friendship in his old fashion to the garden, to his mother, to the many-colored stones that bordered the beds.

But then came a spring that did not sound and smell like all the earlier ones; the blackbird sang and it was not the old song, the blue iris bloomed and no dreams or fairy tales drifted out and in along the gold-fenced pathway of its chalice. Strawberries in hiding laughed from among the green shadows, butterflies tumbled magnificently above the woodbine, but nothing was any longer the way it had always been; the boy had other interests, and he was frequently at odds with his mother. He himself did not know what the trouble was or why it hurt so, why something was always bothering him. He only saw that the world had changed, that the friendships of earlier times had fallen away and left him alone.

Thus a year passed, and then another, and Anselm was no longer a child. The colored stones around the flower-beds bored him, the flowers were silent, and he kept the beetles in a case, impaled on pins. The old joys had dried up and withered, and his soul had begun the long hard detour.

Boisterously the young man made his way into life, which seemed to him to have just begun. Blown away and forgotten was the world of allegory; new desires and new paths enticed him. The aura of childhood still lingered about him, in his blue eyes and soft hair, but he was irritated when reminded of it and had his hair cut short and adopted as bold and worldly an air as he could muster. Unpredictable, he stormed through the troubling second-ary-school years, sometimes a good student and friend, sometimes alone and withdrawn, now buried in books until late at night, now wild and obstreperous at his first youthful drinking bouts. He had had to leave home and saw it only on very brief occasions when he came to visit his mother. Greatly changed, grown tall, handsomely dressed, he would bring friends or books with him, always different ones, and when he walked through the old garden, it was small and silent under his distraught glance. He no longer read stories in the many-colored veins of the stones and the leaves, he no longer saw God and eternity dwelling in the blue secrecy of the iris blossom.

Anselm went to secondary school, then to college; he came home with a red cap and then with a yellow one, with fuzz on his upper lip and then with a youthful beard. He brought books in foreign languages with him and one time a dog, and in a letter case in his breast pocket he sometimes carried secret poems, the sayings of ancient wise men, or pictures of pretty girls and letters from them. He came back from travels in distant lands and from sea voyages on great ships. He came back again and was a young teacher, wearing a black hat and dark gloves, and his old neighbors tipped their hats to him and called him professor although he was not yet that. Once more he came, wearing black clothes, and walked slim and solemn behind the slowly moving hearse in which his old mother lay in a flower-covered coffin. And after that he seldom returned.

In the metropolis where Anselm was now a teacher and had a high academic reputation, he went about behaving exactly like other people of the world. He wore a fine hat and coat, he was serious or genial as the occasion demanded, he observed the world with alert but rather weary eyes, and he was a gentleman and a scholar just as he had wanted to be. But now things took a new turn for him, very much as they had at the end of his childhood. He suddenly felt as if many years had slipped past and left him standing strangely alone and unsatisfied with a way of life for which he had always longed. It was no real happiness to be a professor, it was not really gratifying to be respectfully greeted by citizens and students, it was all stale and commonplace. Happiness once more lay far in the future and the road there looked hot and dusty and tiresome.

At this time Anselm often visited the house of a friend whose sister he found attractive. He was no longer inclined to run after pretty faces; in this too he had changed, and he felt that happiness for him must come in some special fashion and was not to be expected behind every window. His friend's sister pleased him greatly and often he thought he truly loved her. But she was a strange girl; her every gesture, every word, bore her own stamp and coloring, and it was not always easy to keep pace with her in exactly the same rhythm. Evenings when Anselm walked up and down in his lonely home, reflectively listening to his own footsteps echoing through the empty rooms, he struggled a great deal within himself about this woman. She was older than he would have wished his wife to be. She was odd, and it would be difficult to live with her and pursue his academic ambitions, with which she had no sympathy at all. Also she was not very robust or healthy and in particular could not easily endure company and parties. By preference she lived in lonely quiet amid flowers, music, and books, letting the world go its way or come to her if it must. Sometimes her sensitivity was so acute that when something alien wounded her she would burst into tears. Then again she would glow with some silent and secret happiness, and anyone who saw her would think how difficult it would be to give anything to this strange beautiful woman or to mean anything to her. Sometimes Anselm believed she loved him, sometimes it seemed to him that she loved no one but was simply gentle and friendly with everyone and wanted nothing but to be left in peace. But he demanded something quite different from life, and if he were to marry, then there must be life and excitement and hospitality in his home.

"Iris," he said to her, "dear Iris, if only the world were differently arranged! If nothing at all existed but your beautiful gentle world of flowers, thoughts, and music, then I too would wish for nothing at all but to spend my whole life with you, to hear your stories and to share in your thoughts. Your very name does me good. Iris is a wonderful name, and I have no idea what it reminds me of."

"But you do know," she said, "that the blue and yellow sword lilies are called that."

"Yes," he replied with an uneasy feeling. "I know it very well and that in itself is beautiful. But always when I pronounce your name it seems to remind me of something else, I don't know what, as though it were connected with some very deep, distant, important memories, and yet I don't know what they might be and cannot seem to find out."

Iris smiled at him as he stood there at a loss, rubbing his forehead with his hand.

"I always feel the same way," she said to Anselm in her light, birdlike voice, "whenever I smell a flower. My heart feels as though a memory of something completely beautiful and precious were bound up with the fragrance, something that was mine a long time ago and that I have lost. It is that way too with music and sometimes with poems— suddenly there is a flash for an instant as though all at once I saw a lost homeland lying below in the valley, but instantly it is gone again and forgotten. Dear Anselm, I believe we are on earth for this purpose, for this contemplation and seeking and listening for lost, far-off strains, and behind them lies our true home."

"How beautifully you put it," he said admiringly, and he felt an almost painful stirring in his breast, as though a compass hidden there were persistently pointing toward his distant goal. But that goal was quite different from the one he had deliberately set for his life, which disturbed him, for was it, after all, worthy of him to squander his life in dreams with only pretty fairy tales for pretext?

And one day Herr Anselm came back from one of his lonely journeys and found his barren scholar's quarters so chilly and oppressive that he rushed off to his friend's house, determined to ask beautiful Iris for her hand.

"Iris," he said to her, "I don't want to go on living this way. You have always been my good friend. I must tell you everything. I need a wife, otherwise my life seems empty and meaningless. And whom should I want for a wife but you, my darling flower? Are you willing, Iris? You shall have flowers, as many as we can find, you shall have the most beautiful garden. Are you willing to come to me?"

Iris looked him in the eye calmly and with deliberation; she did not smile, she did not blush, and she answered him in a firm voice.

"Anselm, I am not surprised at your question. You are dear to me, although I had never thought of being your wife. But look, my friend, I demand a great deal from the man I marry. I make greater demands than most women. You offer me flowers and you mean well by it. But I can live even without flowers, and without music too; I could very well do without many other things as well, if it were necessary. But one thing I cannot and will not do without: I can never live so much as a single day in such a way that the music in my heart is not dominant. If I am to live with a man, it must be one whose inner music harmonizes beautifully and exactly with mine, and his single desire must be that his own music be pure and that it blend well with mine. Can you do that, my friend? Very likely you will not become more famous this way or garner further honors, your house will be quiet, and the furrows which I have seen in your brow for many a year must all be smoothed out. Oh, Anselm, it will not work. Look, you are so constituted that you always have to study new furrows into your forehead, constantly create new worries, and what I perceive and am, you no doubt love and find pleasant, but for you as for most people it is after all simply a pretty toy. Oh, listen to me carefully: everything that now seems a toy to you is life itself to me and would have to be so to you too, and everything you strive for and worry about is for me a toy, in my eyes is not worth living for— I shall not change, Anselm, for I live according to an inner law, but will you be able to change? And you would have to change completely if I were to be your wife."

Anselm could not speak, startled by the strength of her will, which he had always thought weak and frivolous. He remained silent and thoughtlessly crushed a flower he had picked up from the table in his nervous hand.

When Iris gently took the flower from him, her action struck him to the heart, like a sharp rebuke—and then suddenly she smiled cheerfully and charmingly, as though she had unexpectedly found a way out of the darkness.

"I have an idea," she said in a gentle voice, and blushed as she spoke. "You will find it strange, it will seem to you a whim. But it is no whim. Will you listen to it? And will you agree that it will decide about you and me?"

Without understanding her, Anselm stared at Iris with worry in his pale features. Her smile compelled him to have confidence and say yes.

"I want to give you a task," Iris said, becoming immediately very serious again.

"Do so, it is your right," Anselm replied.

"This is serious with me," she said, "and it is my last word. Will you accept it as it comes straight from my soul and not quibble or bargain about it, even if you don't understand it right away?"

Anselm promised. Then she said, getting up and giving

him her hand: "Often you have said to me that whenever you speak my name you are reminded of a forgotten something that was once important and holy in your eyes. That is a sign, Anselm, and it is what has drawn you to me all these years. I too believe you have lost and forgotten something important and holy in your soul, something that must be reawakened before you can find happiness and attain what is intended for you. —Farewell, Anselm! I give you my hand and I beg you: go and make sure you find again in your memory what it is you are reminded of by my name. On the day when you have rediscovered that, I will go with you as your wife wherever you wish and have no desires but yours."

In confusion and dismay, Anselm tried to interrupt her and dismiss this demand as a whim, but with one bright look she reminded him of his promise and he fell silent. With lowered eyes he took her hand, raised it to his lips, and left.

In the course of his life he had taken upon himself many tasks and had carried them out, but none had been so strange, important, and at the same time dismaying as this one. Day after day he hurried around concentrating on it until he was weary, and the time always came when in despair and anger he denounced the whole undertaking as a crazy feminine notion and rejected it completely. But then something deep within him disagreed, a very faint secret pain, a soft, scarcely audible warning. This low voice, which was in his own heart, acknowledged that Iris was right and it made the same demand that she did.

However, the task was much too difficult for this man

of learning. He was supposed to remember something he had long ago forgotten, he was to find once more a single golden thread in the fabric of the sunken years, he was to grasp with his hands and deliver to his beloved something that was no more than a vanished bird song, an impulse of joy or sorrow on hearing a piece of music, something finer, more fleeting and bodiless than a thought, more insubstantial than a dream, as formless as morning mist.

Sometimes when he had abandoned the search and given up in bad temper, unexpectedly something like a breath from a distant garden touched him, he whispered the name Iris to himself ten times and more, softly and lightly, like one testing a note on a tight string. "Iris," he whispered, "Iris," and with a faint pain he felt something stir within him, the way in an old abandoned house a door swings open without reason or a cupboard creaks. He went over his memories, which he had believed to be stored away in good order, and made amazing and startling discoveries. His treasury of memories was a great deal smaller than he would have surmised. Whole years were missing, and when he thought back they stood there as empty as blank pages. He found that he had great difficulty in summoning up a clear image of his mother. He had completely forgotten the name of a girl whom as a youth he had hotly courted for a whole year. He happened to remember a dog he had once purchased on the spur of the moment and had kept with him for a time; it took him a whole day to recall the dog's name.

Painfully, with increasing sorrow and fear, the poor fellow saw how wasted and empty was the life that lay behind him, no longer belonging to him, alien and with no relationship to himself, like something once learned by heart of which one could now only with difficulty retrieve meaningless fragments. He began to write; he wanted to set down, going backward year by year, his most important experiences so as to have them clearly in mind again. But what had been his most important experiences? When he had been appointed professor? When he had received his doctorate, been an undergraduate, been a secondary-school student? Or when once in the forgotten past this girl or that had for a time pleased him? He looked up terrified: Was this life? Was this all? He struck himself on the forehead and laughed bitterly.

Meanwhile, time ran on, never had it fled so inexorably! A year was gone and it seemed to him that he was in exactly the same position as when he had left Iris. Yet in this time he had greatly changed, as everyone except himself recognized. He had become almost a stranger to his acquaintances, he was considered absentminded, peevish, and odd, he gained a reputation of being an unpredictable eccentric—too bad about him, but he had been a bachelor too long. There were times when he forgot his academic duties and his students waited for him in vain. Deep in thought, he would sometimes prowl through the streets, brushing the housefronts and the dust from the windowsills with his threadbare coat as he passed. Many thought that he had begun to drink. But at other times he would stop in the midst of a classroom lecture, attempting to recall something; his face would break into an appealing, childlike smile in a manner entirely new to him, and then he would go on talking with a warmth of feeling that touched many of his listeners to the heart.

In the course of his hopeless search for some continuity among the faint traces of bygone years, he had acquired a new faculty of which he was not aware. It happened more and more frequently that behind what he had hitherto called memories there lay other memories, much as on an old wall painted with ancient pictures still older ones have been overpainted and lie hidden and unsuspected. He would try to recall something, perhaps the name of a city where he had once spent some days on his travels, or the birthday of a friend, or anything at all, and while he was burrowing and searching through a little piece of the past as though through rubble, suddenly something entirely different would occur to him. A breath would unexpectedly reach him like an April morning breeze or a September mist. He smelled a fragrance, tasted a flavor, felt delicate dark sensations here and there, on his skin, in his eyes, in his heart, and slowly it came to him that there must once have been a day, blue and warm or cool and gray, or whatever kind of day, and the essence of it must have been caught within him and clung there as a buried memory. He could not place in the real past that spring or winter day he distinctly smelled and felt, he could attach no name or date to it; perhaps it had been during his college days, perhaps, even, he had been in the cradle, but the fragrance was there and he knew that something lived in him which he did not recognize and could not identify or define. Sometimes it seemed to him as though these memories might well reach back beyond life into a former existence, although he would smile at the thought.

Anselm discovered a good deal in his helpless wanderings through the abysses of memory. He found much that touched and gripped him, and much that startled him and filled him with terror, but the one thing he did not find was what the name Iris meant to him. In the torment of his fruitless search he went once to explore his old home, saw the woods and the streets, the footpaths and fences, stood in the old garden of his childhood and felt the waves break over his heart, the past encompassing him like a dream. Saddened and silent, he returned and with the announcement that he was ill he had everyone who wanted to see him turned away.

One, however, insisted on entering, the friend he had not seen since his courtship of Iris had ended. This friend found Anselm sitting unkempt in his cheerless study.

"Get up," he said to him, "and come with me. Iris wants to see you."

Anselm sprang to his feet.

"Iris! What has happened to her? —Oh, I know, I know!"

"Yes," said his friend, "come with me. She is going to die. She has been ill for a long time."

They went to Iris, who was lying on a sofa, slender and light as a child. She smiled luminously with overlarge eyes and gave Anselm her light white childlike hand, which lay like a flower in his. Her face was as though transfigured.

"Anselm," she said, "are you angry with me? I set you a

hard task and I see that you have remained faithful. Go on searching, go on as you have been doing until you find what you are looking for. You thought you were searching on my account but you were doing it for yourself. Do you realize that?"

"I suspected it," Anselm said, "and now I know it. It is a vast journey, Iris, and I would long since have turned back, but now I can find no way to do that. I don't know what is to become of me."

She gazed deep into his sorrowful eyes and smiled encouragingly; he bent over her thin hand and wept in silence, and her hand became wet with his tears.

"What is to become of you?" she said in a voice that was only like a glow of memory. "What is to become of you is something you must not ask. You have sought many things in your life. You have sought honor and happiness and knowledge and you have sought me, your little Iris. All these were only pretty pictures and they deserted you, as I must now desert you. It has been the same with me. What I sought always turned out to be dear and lovely pictures and they always failed and faded. Now I have no more pictures, I seek nothing more, I am returning home and have only one small step to take and then I shall be in my native land. You too will join me there, Anselm, and then you will have no more furrows in your brow."

She was so pale that Anselm cried out in despair: "Oh, wait, Iris, do not go yet. Leave me some sign that you are not disappearing completely."

She nodded and reached over to a vase beside her and gave him a fresh, full-blown blue sword lily.

"Here, take my flower, the iris, and do not forget me. Search for me, search for the iris, then you will come to me."

Weeping, Anselm held the flower in his hands and weeping took his leave. When a message from his friend summoned him, he returned and helped adorn Iris's coffin with flowers and lower it into the earth.

Then his life fell to pieces around him; it seemed impossible for him to go on spinning this thread. He gave everything up, left his position and the city, and disappeared from the world. Here and there he turned up briefly. He was seen in his native town leaning over the fence of the old flower garden, but when people inquired after him and wanted to assist him he was nowhere to be found.

The sword lily remained dear to him. Whenever he came upon one, he would bend over it and sink his gaze into the calyx for a long time and out of the bluish depths a fragrance and a presentiment of all that had been and was to be seemed to be rising toward him, until sadly he went his way because fulfillment did not come. It was as though he were listening at a half-open door and behind it the most enchanting secret was being breathed, and just when he felt that at that very moment everything would be made plain to him and would be fulfilled, the door swung shut and the chill wind of the world blew over his loneliness.

In his dreams his mother spoke to him; her face and form he had not seen so close and clear for many long years. And Iris spoke to him, and when he awoke, an echo lingered in his ears to which he would devote a whole day of thought. He had no permanent abode. He hurried through the country like a stranger, slept in houses or in the woods, ate bread or berries, drank wine or the dew from the leaves of bushes, but was oblivious to it all. Some took him for a fool, some for a magician, some feared him, some laughed at him, many loved him. He acquired skills he had never had before, like being with children and taking part in their strange games, or holding conversations with a broken twig or a little stone. Winters and summers raced by him, he kept looking into the chalices of flowers and into brooks and lakes.

"Pictures," he said at times to himself, "everything just pictures."

But within him he felt an essence that was not a picture and this he followed, and the essence within him at times would speak, and its voice was the voice of Iris and the voice of his mother, and it was comfort and hope.

Wonders came his way but did not surprise him. For example, one winter day he was walking through the snow in an open field, ice forming in his beard. There in the snow stood slim and pointed an iris stalk which bore a single beautiful blossom. He bent over to it and smiled, for now he realized what it was that Iris had again and again urged him to remember. He recognized his childhood dream when he saw between the golden pickets the light-blue, brightly veined path leading into the secret heart of the flower, and he knew that this was what he sought, that this was the essence and not any longer a picture.

And presentiments came to him again, dreams guided

him, and he found a hut where children gave him milk, and as he played with them they told him stories; they told him that in the forest near the charcoal burners' huts a miracle had occurred. There the spirit gate had been seen standing open, the gate that opens only once in a thousand years. He listened and nodded assent to the cherished picture and went on, a bird in an alder bush sang in front of him, a bird with a strange sweet note like the voice of the dead Iris. He followed the bird as it flew and hopped ahead of him, deep into the forest.

When the bird fell silent and disappeared, Anselm stopped and looked about him. He was standing in a deep valley in the forest, water ran softly under broad green leaves; otherwise, all was silent as if full of expectation. But in Anselm's breast the bird continued to sing with the beloved voice and it urged him on until he stood in front of a cliff overgrown with moss, and in the middle of it was a gaping fissure that led narrowly into the interior of the mountain.

In front of the fissure sat an old man who arose when he saw Anselm approaching and cried: "You there, turn back! This is the spirit gate. No one has ever returned who entered here."

Anselm glanced up and into the rocky entrance. There he saw a blue path disappearing deep inside the mountain and golden pillars stood close together along both sides and the path within led downward as though into the chalice of an enormous flower.

In his breast rose the bird's clear song and Anselm strode past the guardian into the fissure and between the golden columns into the blue mystery of the interior. It was Iris into whose heart he entered, and it was the sword lily in his mother's garden into whose blue chalice he softly strode, and as he silently drew closer to the golden twilight all memory and all knowledge were suddenly at his command, he felt of his hand and found it small and soft, voices of love sounded near and familiar in his ears, and the ring they had and the glow of the golden columns were like the ring and glow everything had had at that distant time in the springtide of his childhood.

And the dream he had dreamed as a small boy was his again, that he was striding into the chalice, and behind him the whole world of images strode too and glided and sank into the mystery that lies behind all images.

Softly Anselm began to sing, and his path sloped gently downward into his homeland.